"To me," she toasted

"And to the marvelously adaptable man I married."
Unable to find wineglasses, she had set out water
tumblers, and she poured a full glass of the sparkling
beverage, holding it high in the air. "May the rest of
our marriage be carried out as far from each other as
possible." Stacey clicked her glass against the empty
one sitting on the crate. "Here's to you, Ryan," she
said, draining the entire glass in one long series of
swallows.

The wine affected her empty stomach like a meteor
shower. That's better, she thought with satisfaction.
The new feeling gave her something to think about
other than her misery. If one glass made her feel that
different, two should feel even better. She quickly
drained another glass. "Better still," she muttered.

Dear Reader,

Although our culture is always changing, the desire to love and be loved is a constant in every woman's heart. Silhouette Romances reflect that desire, sweeping you away with books that will make you laugh and cry, poignant stories that will move you time and time again.

This summer we're featuring Romances with a playful twist. Remember those fun-loving heroines who always manage to get themselves into tricky predicaments? You'll enjoy reading about their escapades in Silhouette Romances by Brittany Young, Debbie Macomber, Annette Broadrick and Rita Rainville.

We're also publishing Romances by many of your all-time favorites such as Ginna Gray, Dixie Browning, Laurie Paige and Joan Hohl. Your overwhelming reaction to these authors has served as a touchstone for us, and we're pleased to bring you more books with Silhouette's distinctive medley of charm, wit and—above all—*romance*. I hope you enjoy this book, and the many stories to come.

Sincerely,

Rosalind Noonan
Senior Editor
SILHOUETTE BOOKS

EMILIE RICHARDS
Sweet
Georgia Gal

Silhouette Romance

Published by Silhouette Books New York

America's Publisher of Contemporary Romance

SILHOUETTE BOOKS
300 E. 42nd St., New York, N.Y. 10017

Copyright © 1985 by Emilie McGee

Distributed by Pocket Books

ISBN: 0-373-08393-9

First Silhouette Books printing October 1985

10 9 8 7 6 5 4 3 2 1

America's Publisher of Contemporary Romance

Printed in the U.S.A.

Books by Emilie Richards

Silhouette Romance

Brendan's Song #372
Sweet Georgia Gal #393

EMILIE RICHARDS

grew up in St. Petersburg and attended college in northern Florida. She also fell in love there, and married her husband, Michael, who is her opposite in every way. "The only thing we agreed on was that we were very much in love. We haven't changed our minds about that in the sixteen years we've been together." They now live in New Orleans with four children, who span the years from toddler to teenager.

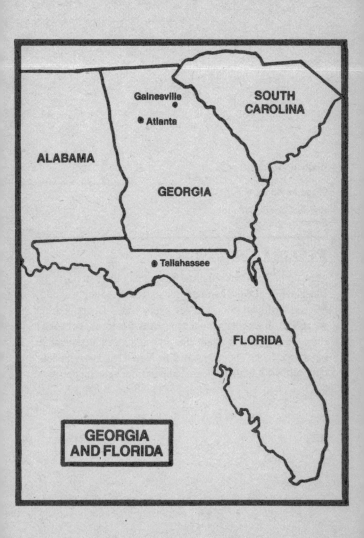

GEORGIA
AND FLORIDA

Chapter One

The young woman surrounded by laughing children on the front porch swing was a Norman Rockwell painting brought to life. A graceful green-and-white checked dress billowed around her slim ankles as the swing rocked back and forth. The gingham print was almost lost under a ruffled white eyelet apron embroidered with delicate yellow daisies, and one of the children had made a matching circlet of real daisies, setting it on the woman's head like a crown. The scene spoke of simpler days, of lazy summer afternoons and basic, wholesome pleasures. If there were jet planes flying overhead and the faint sounds of a vacuum cleaner in the background, they were hardly noticeable.

But Stacey MacDonald was not conscious of the impression she and the children were making. She was listening carefully to the sweet cadences of their voices, and she was glorying in them. Not since she had sat on a similar front porch and traded stories with her own younger brothers and sisters had she felt so relaxed.

The sunlight streamed down, sending hot, shimmering rays to dance over the porch and to caress the darkly golden hues of her hair. Individual strands escaped the tight constraints of a fluffy ponytail and left curly tendrils framing her face and the soft planes of her neck. The strands tickled, and Stacey absentmindedly brushed them away as she pulled the youngest child onto her lap for a hug.

The children, too, were dressed as from another era: checked shirts and overalls and frilly, long, Kate Greenaway party dresses replaced their usual Star Wars T-shirts and cut-offs. The girls tried valiantly to keep their hands away from their hair ribbons, and their brother, with the good manners of another generation, was trying not to fidget too much. Their conversation, however, was strictly late twentieth century.

"Stacey, will you come see my all-star soccer game next week? I'm going to be goalie." The loaded swing was rocking frantically now as the conversation escalated. "Stop shouting, it's my turn!" "Do you like my hair, Stacey? I wanted to get it cut real short like that punk singer on TV, but Mommy wouldn't let me." "Move over Heidi, or I'll..."

"Kids, scoot. You're going to wear Stacey out before the party even starts." Margie Finlaw pushed through the half-open screen door and lovingly shoved her brood off the swing. With a tired sigh, she flopped into the now-available seat next to Stacey, her long yellow cotton skirt settling around her. "Go tell your father that it's time to put the barbecue sauce on the pig."

Stacey hugged the smallest Finlaw again and waved as the children, tripping over each other, scampered down the porch steps. Turning, she surveyed her cousin, large hazel eyes solemn. "You didn't have to do that, Margie. You know how I feel about your kids."

"I know that given half a chance, you'll spend your time with the children instead of the grown-ups at this party. I'm sworn to protect you from yourself." Margie waved her hand to stir the air in front of her. She succeeded only in further tousling her short brown hair, but somehow, with Margie, tousled was to be expected and looked perfectly appropriate. "Tallahassee in the summertime is really only fit for quiet indoor conversation. Why am I having this shindig? Who ever heard of an old-fashioned pig roast in this heat?"

"You're having it because you love it, and you know it." Stacey turned her head and happily surveyed the green acres surrounding the old white farmhouse. Everywhere she looked, huge live oaks and pecan trees provided welcome shade for the house and yard. Beds of flowers growing in riotous, random patterns zigzagged across the lawn and along the seemingly endless driveway. In the distance, a blue pond sparkled behind an ancient, collapsing barn. "I'm so glad you invited me, Margie. I love being here. I've been so busy finishing up my final quarter that it seems like forever since I've seen you."

"Ron has kept me posted as to your health and welfare. At least as your college adviser he gets to keep track of you." Margie reached over and tucked a strand of hair back into Stacey's ponytail. "Are you glad to finally be all done with school?"

"Absolutely delighted. I feel as if my life has been on hold for the last five years. As much as I loved it, I'm ready to get on with other things." She stretched her arms over her head, revealing the graceful, feminine lines of her body. "Now all I have to do is find a teaching job for next fall."

Margie gave the younger woman an encouraging smile. "That shouldn't be too hard with your credentials. Terrific grades—" She laughed at Stacey's pinkening cheeks. "Come on, you can't hide your accomplishments from me, I'm married to your adviser. Terrific grades and a love of children that won't quit."

Accepting compliments embarrassed Stacey. Deftly she changed the subject. "Well, jobs are few and far between, as I'm finding out, no matter how well qualified I am. I'll just have to see what turns up. In the meantime, I'm going to start looking for a summer job tomorrow."

"Well, I always thought that resourceful was your middle name." Margie stood, holding out a hand to Stacey. "Since you're here early, I'm assuming that means you want to help me set up."

"Change my middle name to dependable." Stacey followed Margie through the squeaking screen door. "What major jobs did you save for me?" she teased.

"Sometimes it just doesn't pay to have a younger cousin hanging around." Margie stuck her tongue out. "Just be careful, or I'll start trotting out some old tales from your childhood."

"My childhood was impeccable."

"Ah...but your adolescence!"

The living room of the renovated farmhouse was a jumble of puzzles, children's toys, and comfortable furniture. Without thinking, Stacey began to straighten up and sort toys, placing them neatly on available shelves and in discreet piles behind furniture. "What tales could you possibly tell of my adolescence? I was in Georgia and you were married and living here in Florida by then."

"I followed the lives of the entire MacDonald clan with the help of weekly reports from my mother. Mama was so delighted to have someone to gossip to long distance. Let's see, I seem to remember a story about you and some boy getting sent home in disgrace from a hayride."

"The scandal of my life," Stacey said, feigning a swoon as she collapsed onto the sofa to begin assembling puzzle pieces. "The boy actually kissed me in front of the good pastor of his church."

"Your first and last kiss?"

Stacey grabbed a pillow and shot it expertly at Margie's head. "Wouldn't you like to know?"

"I've seen the hungry young men nipping at your heels like a pack of wild dogs. I'm just keeping you on the straight and narrow," Margie said sweetly. "After all, if you really are going to get on with your life, so to speak, you'll need to be cautious."

"Virtuous, maidenly, and innocent beyond all reason," Stacey recited, only half in jest. "I'm a regular Rebecca of Sunnybrook Farm."

"It seems to me that I've heard a much more scandalous description of you. Let's see—how did it go?"

Striking a pose as Stacey moaned, Margie began to intone in a singsong voice with the solemnity of a radio announcer: "Hair the color of wildflower honey; eyes the changing colors of a mountain autumn; skin like peaches and cream; lips like a sweet watermelon. Gainesville's candidate for Miss Georgia, Stacey MacDonald, has a wholesome beauty that is perfectly at home in blue jeans or on an auditorium stage in a formfitting swimsuit."

Stacey kept her head down as she attempted to be casual. "How you can remember that old newspaper article verbatim is beyond me. And besides, it wasn't true. I wasn't at home parading in a swimsuit at all. To this day, I still tremble in protest when I have to wear one."

Margie caught the seriousness in Stacey's voice and stopped teasing. Since Stacey had come to live in Tallahassee and attend Florida State University where Margie's husband was a professor, the two women had gone from just being part of an extensive network of relatives to becoming close friends. The ten-year age difference hardly seemed to matter, and Margie understood Stacey as only a friend who shares a common background can. "Knowing you, I'll bet all that hoop-de-do was pretty hard to take," she responded with sympathy.

"It was very hard to take at times, but the Miss Georgia pageant helped get me through college."

Margie dropped a hand on Stacey's shoulder. "You know, honey, everybody is so proud of you. You're the first MacDonald kid to get a degree."

A smile lit Stacey's face and she lifted her head. "The first of many, I hope. But thanks, Margie."

"Can you finish up here? I'm going to check the upstairs bathroom and make sure it's clean. Introduce yourself to anyone who comes along."

Stacey wandered across the room, fluffing pillows and smoothing the throw covers on the furniture. Margie's home was almost as familiar to her as the house she had grown up in. Indeed, the houses were two of a kind—with one important difference. Stacey's childhood home, a big, rambling farmhouse, had been largely untouched since its construction except for new rooms added helter-skelter style as the MacDonald kid count neared its present even dozen.

In contrast, Margie's house had been renovated by a master hand, retaining its country ambience while reaching for the contemporary luxuries of open space and greater access to the outdoors. For Stacey, being there was a treat, a welcome respite from her own tiny apartment where the walls sometimes seemed to close in around her.

Car horns and laughter sounded from outside, and when she had finished straightening up she wandered out to the front porch to survey the arriving guests. Some were students whom she knew from Ron Finlaw's classes, and others were colleagues of his. Owners of neighboring farms arrived, bringing swarms of shouting children, and soon the party was in full swing.

Not everyone was in costume. There was the usual college crowd who favored cut-offs and T-shirts for every occasion, but most of the guests had tried to coordinate their attire to the old-fashioned theme of the party. Stacey was swept into the high-spirited crowd, and only after she had taken some time to talk to everyone she knew or was introduced to did she manage to excuse herself to find out whether Margie needed any more help.

The living room was still neat and obviously undiscovered by the horde of children at the party. On the wall facing the oak stairway was a collection of old portraits, and Stacey, who had been too busy before, noticed a new addition to the series of unsmiling men and women that Margie treasured so much. Moving over to inspect it, she failed to see the small child tucked away under the glass-topped coffee table. It was only after she tripped over a tiny foot that she realized that she was not alone.

"Well, sweetheart, I'm so sorry," she said to the top of the curly blond head. She knelt down in front of the picture-book-pretty little girl. "Did I hurt you?"

No answer except gentle sobs echoed from under the coffee table.

Without thinking twice, Stacey reached underneath the table and pulled the half-resisting body toward her. "We can't have you crying all by yourself, honey. Can I see your toe?"

The little girl continued to cry as Stacey inspected the tiny pink toes encased in miniature white sandals. "I think you'll be fine, but I'll just bet that hurts, doesn't it? Let's see if we can find your mother." Her words set off a new wave of tears, and Stacey picked the child up and cuddled her close. The little body seemed lighter than the air surrounding it, and Stacey, used to the sturdy bodies of her own country-born-and-bred brothers and sisters, was shocked by the fragility of this one. "Goodness, child," she murmured, "let's get you something to eat."

The screen door banged shut and Stacey, still cuddling the now quiet child, turned to inspect the newcomer. Standing in the doorway was a man she didn't know—of that she was certain. This was a man she would never have forgotten. Taller than average, his raw-boned frame seemed to eclipse the doorway, sending the light that was streaming in behind him skittering in diffuse patterns around the room.

His hair was rich chocolate with reddish glints that highlighted the out-of-control curls falling over his forehead. Tanned and powerful, with snapping, heavy-lidded brown eyes, he was the image of male virility and health. To top off the impression of raw masculinity, he was dressed in a flowing homespun shirt—Mississippi-riverboatman style—slit halfway down his chest. Faded, frayed jeans hugged his slim waist and well-shaped thighs. His bare feet were dark and surprisingly clean. Perhaps when Tom Sawyer or Huck Finn grew to manhood, leaving all traces of boyishness behind, he would have looked like this man.

I have stared long enough, Stacey told herself. But the truth was that forever would not have been long enough. She knew immediately, without wanting to know it, that in some indefinable way this man was weaving himself into her being. And to Stacey, too busy most of her life to dream romantic dreams, that knowledge was knee-knocking frightening. For that reason alone, it was time to break the spell.

Her decision to put an end to her own assessment was evidently not echoed by the man. He was giving her a long, slow perusal that had reached only as far as the scooped neckline of her dress, and she was suddenly aware that one of the things he would see was her skin turning a healthy pink. She grasped at the first thing she could think of to stop his investigation.

"Excuse me, do you know whose child this is?" The voice that emerged was level and polite. What astonished Stacey was the fact that her natural Georgia accent, which had been slipping away during the last five years, had returned with a vengeance. I am not playing the Southern belle, she told herself fiercely. I am not pretending to be Scarlett O'Hara.

"Yes; she belongs to me." The investigation was over; his heavy-lidded eyes were focused on hers with a trace of amusement.

If the child was his, why hadn't he stepped forward to claim her? And if the child was his...he was a married man. So much for brief, potent, romantic daydreams. She solved the problem of hiding her disappointment by turning her face down to the little girl's. "I'm afraid I stepped on her foot. She was hiding under the table, but she's all right now. Aren't you, sweetie?" she asked the child.

The child, who seemed to respond to questions only by weeping, lay passively in Stacey's arms. Confused by the little girl's lack of interest in returning to her father, Stacey moved across the room to place her in his arms. He reached for the child, and in a dizzying moment of contact, his arms partially closed around Stacey as they made the transfer. She could feel the warmth radiating from his body and the brush of his arms as he scooped the child from against her breasts. The heat that surged inside her had nothing to do with the summer afternoon.

For the little girl, the exchange precipitated a fresh wave of sobs. And surprisingly, the man, for all his masculine charms, seemed to have no idea of what to do with a child. Awkwardly, as if he had had no practice, the man held the sobbing little girl against his shoulder. "There, there, Christy," he soothed helplessly. "There, there."

Stacey backed quickly away. "I think I'd better leave you two alone," she said softly, glad to make her escape. Up close, married or not, the man was far too attractive.

"Please, don't!"

What was this magnificent male creature afraid of? The little girl seemed to be about two years old, and yet her father, a man thirty years older, seemed completely unable to cope with her. With a sigh Stacey edged slightly closer again. "I'm sure she's all right," she said to encourage him. "She's probably just a little shaken up."

The man grinned at her, a heart-stopping grin that lit up his features like a sunrise. "She's not the only one," he murmured.

That makes three of us, Stacey thought, panicking internally. Unbeknownst to her, her body, on a hot tip from her subconscious, was inching closer to the father-daughter duo as if to give them the benefit of her calm presence—and, if truth were told, to revel once again in the warmth and heat of this grown-up Mark Twain character.

What in the sweet world are you doing? she reminded herself as she promptly called a halt to her movement. This man had a child. This man was obviously married. This man was extraordinarily dangerous.

"Did you find Christy yet?" A girl's voice sounded from the door. "Oh, there she is. Come here, Christy. Heidi Finlaw's going to take us to see the puppies."

Although at least eight years separated the two girls, there was no question about their shared parentage. Both were graced with the same curly, white-blond hair and enormous blue eyes. It didn't take much insight to see that someday their father was going to have to fight the local boys off with fire hoses.

With a small cry Christy shed her passivity like a snake in springtime and jumped out of the man's arms to run to the girl in the doorway. Without a word to anyone, the older girl picked Christy up, settled her firmly on her hip, and disappeared out the door.

Stacey, who was still standing only inches from the man, looked up at him in startled disbelief.

But the scene was evidently a familiar one to the man. He was obviously less concerned about it than Stacey was, for he appeared to have shrugged it off and once again had begun his examination of her, this time up close.

"Well, now that the crisis has been averted, I'd better see if Margie needs any help," she drawled. Where on earth was that accent coming from? Never a bit ashamed of her roots in Georgia's good red clay, she had never felt that she ought to milk them for all they were worth either. What was he doing to her?

"Thanks for your help." Casually he lifted his large hand and laid a strong, tapering finger against the side of her face. "Does the blush come with the costume, or is it natural?"

"Twentieth-century women don't blush?" she asked in a choked voice, acutely aware of the feather-light touch of his finger on her cheek and the unspoken embrace hinted at in his warm brown eyes.

"Not a one that I've met. It's quite charming, really. Perhaps we can see about bringing it back into style."

"You see about that, I'll see about Margie," she said, forcing herself to turn away from him. Carefully she picked her way across the floor and out the front door to pretend to search for her cousin, who she knew full well was probably in the kitchen. Somehow fresh air seemed more imperative than honesty.

Following the sounds of laughter, Stacey ambled down a path, her long skirts shortening her usually quick stride. A wave of heat assaulted her as she approached the hand-dug barbecue pit, complete now with huge pieces of fragrant pork dripping fat and spicy sauce onto the coals. She deposited a quick kiss on Ron Finlaw's scholarly cheek, heated now from tending the fire, and exchanged some pleasantries with him before allowing a glass of icy lemonade to be pushed into her hand. Lowering herself onto a patchwork quilt, she chatted half-heartedly with friends as she mentally ran through her brief minutes in the living room.

Why had she reacted so strongly to that particular man? She had seen plenty of good-looking, much more available men in her twenty-three years. Why was this one's presence such a feast to her senses? And why, if she was finally going to experience such an instant attraction, something she had given up fantasizing about years before, was she experiencing it for a man who was already taken? Try as she might to talk herself out of the magnetic pull she had felt, she couldn't forget the touch of the man's finger on her face.

Margie joined them, introducing Stacey to the few people she hadn't met yet. There was only one person at the party now whose name Stacey still didn't know. And he was nowhere in sight.

"Has Ryan arrived yet?" A faculty wife had addressed her question to Margie.

Margie waved her hand casually in the air. "He's here somewhere with the kids."

"Ryan?" Stacey tried to sound casual.

"Ryan Cunningham. You know, the architect who helped us renovate the house." Margie was instantly enveloped in a discussion of the relative merits of renovation as opposed to restoration.

Ryan Cunningham. The fair-haired boy of Florida architecture. Stacey sat back and let her mind pull together what little information she had stored there about him, for there was simply no question in her mind now that the man in Margie's living room had been Ryan Cunningham. Not only was he the only man at the party whom she didn't know, he had the same larger-than-life presence that was rumored to surround the famous architect.

Ryan Cunningham. A native of Tallahassee, one of its own grown fat and famous. Ryan Cunningham, a name whispered in the same breath as that of Frank Lloyd Wright. The man who had designed buildings to enhance and blend with the environment in such unique ways that he was now in demand all over the world.

Ryan Cunningham had helped renovate Ron and Margie's house? The idea seemed incredible for an architect of his renown, but Stacey remembered vaguely that Margie had once told her that Ron and Ryan had grown up together, had been next-door neighbors, in fact. Margie had mentioned him only casually, and although Stacey had spent many hours in the Finlaws' presence, she had never run across Ryan Cunningham there. There was one other fact that tickled the far limits of her memory. Somewhere she had heard that there had been a recent tragedy in his life. More than that she couldn't remember.

Margie, who couldn't sit still under the best of circumstances, excused herself in a rustle of yellow skirts and headed back toward the house to finish dinner preparations. Stacey watched her go, still lost in contemplation, until she remembered with a start that the potato salad that she had prepared at home as her contribution to the party was still sitting in an ice chest in her car. Unobtrusively she rose and walked down the long, flower-lined driveway to the gravel road where her little Dodge Colt was parked.

The big glass bowl of potato salad was welcomingly chill against her chest as she started back up to the house. Pushing her way through the screen door, she set the salad down on the dining-room table to open the kitchen door when the sound of a conversation in progress drifted through to her.

"Who's the lush and lovely Georgia peach with the Miss America smile?" drawled the husky male voice that Stacey immediately connected in her mind with dark, curly hair and tanned bare feet. If she was correct, it was the voice of Ryan Cunningham. A few seconds later her conclusion was confirmed.

Stacey recognized Margie's laugh. "Ryan, you have a knack for to-the-point descriptions. You must mean Stacey."

"Lush and lovely, and just ripe for the picking."

Stacey, who had reached for the brass doorknob, drew back as if a rattlesnake were entwined around it.

Margie began scolding him as if he were one of the Finlaw children. "Don't you get any bright ideas, Ryan Cunningham. Stacey MacDonald is not for you. She's as genuine and down-to-earth as cornbread and sorghum molasses. Not your usual type at all."

"And what's my usual type?" Stacey could imagine the teasing look on his face.

"Beautiful, cold, and self-centered," Margie shot back quickly.

"Well, Stacey is certainly beautiful...and I'd have to check out the 'cold' part up close..." The words, meant to provoke Margie, made Stacey's heart take a nose dive into her stomach. Check her out indeed! But somehow the idea wasn't as abhorrent as it should have been.

"Look, Ryan. Girls like Stacey are as rare as a Tallahassee snowstorm." Margie was sputtering now. "She's the kind of girl you have to take home to your mother before you get to take her home to your bedroom. Do I make myself clear?"

Stacey heard a chair squeak across the floor before Ryan's voice sounded from the other side of the room. "What's your interest in this girl, Margie?"

"She's my cousin." The words were said with finality.

"Cousin Stacey. Now I remember you talking about her. Amazing that we haven't met before, considering how much time we both probably spend with you. Could that be a coincidence?"

Stacey didn't stay to find out the answer. She knew Margie; it was not a coincidence. In an age where families lived cities apart and were reunited only for occasional holidays, Stacey and Margie were active members of a minority, a huge, extended family that watched closely over its own. Margie was just doing what was expected of her when she neglected to introduce cousin Stacey to this exceptionally attractive man. Especially since he was already married and apparently on the prowl in spite of it.

Still, Stacey was humiliated by the conversation that she had just eavesdropped on. Hearing herself discussed like a piece of horseflesh that would go only to the bidder with the best qualifications was mortifying and faintly familiar. Memories of standing on a stage and having her worth judged by strangers flooded through her. But while she wanted to hang her head in shame, the fact that this particular stranger found her beautiful was sending electrical impulses down her spine.

"It's time to take a walk," she muttered to herself and, noiselessly closing the screen door, she crossed the porch and started down the steps.

Although she had been in the house only for a short time, it had evidently been long enough for her to miss out on something important. Outside, people had clustered around the front of the house in frantic little huddles. In the middle of the yard, Stacey saw Ryan Cunningham's older daughter, her head in her hands, sobbing. The child was loosely surrounded by adults who seemed unable to make her stop. Without thinking, Stacey crossed to the child and knelt beside her. "What's wrong? Can I help?"

"Find Christy!" the little girl sobbed brokenly.

Looking up, Stacey saw Ryan bearing down on them. Obviously someone had shown the presence of mind to look for him and alert him to the problem. "It's all right, Caroline," he said firmly. "Tell me what happened."

"I had Christy with me, and we were walking down the path. I stopped to talk to Heidi and when I remembered to look for Christy, she was gone."

Perhaps Ryan Cunningham wasn't much of a father, Stacey thought privately, but he did know enough not to scold. "That could happen to anyone, Caroline," he said evenly, with no hint of panic in his voice. Only Stacey, inches away from him, could have detected the fear in his eyes. "Now, where were you when you realized that Christy was gone?"

"Over there." The little girl's hand swept toward the ramshackle barn and the pond. Stacey's heart sank. In a flash, Ryan and everyone standing close enough to hear the ominous words were off and running toward the sparkling water. Only Stacey stayed behind to tend to Caroline's needs.

"Come here, Caroline," she said, firmly guiding the little girl to the wide porch steps. "Sit down and let's figure out exactly what happened." It was as much a maneuver to take the child's mind off the search that was now in full progress as anything else, but Caroline took Stacey seriously and stopped crying.

"We were walking along the path, and I stopped—"

"Let's take it back a little further, honey. What were you doing before you were walking down the path?"

"I took Christy to look at the water, but she was scared, so we started walking back."

Breathing a silent sigh of relief because Christy was afraid of the pond, Stacey continued to probe. "Where had you been before that?"

"To see the puppies."

Ron and Margie were the proud owners of a purebred Australian shepherd, Waltzing Matilda, who had given birth to her first litter of pups the week before. It would make sense, Stacey knew, that Heidi, their oldest daughter, would take the other children to see them. The dog and pups were housed far from the house in an old shed on the east side of the Finlaw property because the mother dog, friendly with family, was snappy with strangers, especially at this time.

"Did Christy like the puppies?" Stacey asked, her heart in her throat.

"She loved them. She cried when we left." There was no need for any more words. Caroline and Stacey took one look at each other, faces aghast, and simultaneously leaped up to begin the long run to the dog shed.

"Caroline," Stacey shouted as her longer legs outdistanced the little girl. "Go back and tell Margie where I am. Tell her to send Ron or to come herself. Matilda will listen to them."

This is too far for a little girl to go, Stacey repeated like a litany. Christy wouldn't know the way. She would be much too afraid to come by herself.

But Stacey knew two-year-olds. She had seen a large number of them emerge in her family, and she knew how determined they could be. There was every chance in the world that Christy had found her way back to the puppies. As she neared the dog's pen, the sharp, angry yapping sound that was Matilda at her fiercest resounded through the air, confirming her worst fears. "Oh, God, let me get there in time," she whispered as she hiked her skirts even higher and put on a new burst of speed.

Rounding the corner, she was brought up short by the sight of her worst visions made real. Christy, frozen to the spot in terror, was standing in the middle of the pen, squirming puppies at her feet and a menacing mother dog slowly stalking her. Waltzing Matilda, obviously upset to have been locked away from her puppies a short time earlier, had lost any trace of her normal good temper. Her growls and her raised hackles were sure signs of her present state of mind.

Stacey, at a loss for any other plan of action, began to talk soothingly to the dog. Although she hadn't been a frequent enough visitor in the last year to qualify as a family member to Matilda, she hoped that the dog would recognize her scent and be calmed by it. "Matilda, baby, it's all right. We aren't going to hurt your puppies. Christy just wanted to see them. There's a good girl." Very slowly, Stacey approached the pen, reached for the gate that Christy had somehow managed to open, and silently pushed her way through.

Matilda was a thin ball of black-and-silver mottled fur, her blue eyes with their characteristically eerie white-spotted pupils darting from side to side. Threatened beyond her canine endurance, she continued to stalk, her body crouched as though ready to spring. But Stacey's calm motions and voice were making inroads in the dog's nervousness. The calculated attack seemed a little less calculated, a little slower. Stacey could almost see the dog thinking over its original defensive strategy.

"There's a good girl," Stacey crooned softly. She was nearing Christy, who luckily was still frozen to the spot, silent tears dripping from her enormous eyes. The child's apparent hopelessness touched Stacey as nothing else ever had. Resolving to throw herself in front of the little body if need be, she began to murmur to the dog, "See? I'm going to pick Christy up and get her out of here."

Very slowly, Stacey reached for the little girl, lifting her beneath her tiny arms and levering her against the bib of the daisy-strewn apron. Wrapping shaking arms around the weightless body, Stacey stood motionless to give the dog a chance to recognize her good intentions. Then slowly she began to back away, careful not to step on the puppies. She continued to chat soothingly to the now still dog.

"Wonderful, Matilda. You're doing fine. We'll be out of here in no time now." Another step backward and another. Stacey calculated that she had only a half dozen more steps to go before she reached the gate when the sound of feet charging down the path reignited the dog's bad temper. With a shrieking growl, Matilda launched herself at Stacey, catching the eyelet apron in her cavernous mouth. Stumbling backward, Stacey managed to keep her foothold as she kicked out at the dog.

"Matilda, no!" Ron's sharp command echoed through Stacey's terror-stricken consciousness, and Matilda, all sweet docility, instantly let go of Stacey's dress. With a whirl, Stacey turned and fled the pen, collapsing directly into Ryan Cunningham's arms.

In an instant, she was encased in his warmth, clutched tightly against his chest as he held her off the ground, which had strangely buckled under her feet. "You're safe now. You and Christy are safe now."

With the strange feeling that if he let her go she would dissolve into a puddle outlined only by green gingham, she remained against him, feeling the comfortable hardness of his chest and the strength of his arms around her. Squeezed between them was Christy, now a wailing ball of curly hair and rumpled pink party dress. Erased from Stacey's mind was the fact that she was allowing someone else's husband to give her the comfort she needed so badly. All that mattered was that his arms remain around her. Indefinitely.

Little by little, feelings returned to her body. Good feelings: some, like relief, that she had experienced before in her life; others, too strange to name. Warmth and life seeped back into her through osmosis from the big man who held her so close. And little by little, with the return to feeling, she realized where she was and who he was. With a sigh she disentangled herself from his embrace. "I think I'm all right now," she murmured. "Thanks for helping me to continue standing."

"The pleasure was mine." With one hand stroking Christy's curls, he cupped his other hand under Stacey's chin, lifting her eyes to his. "We haven't really been introduced. I'm Ryan Cunningham."

"Stacey MacDonald." It was a useless formality. She already had all the information she needed. He was an incredible man. He was also quite unavailable. With another sigh, she realized that during their embrace Christy had not changed hands.

"Christy, go to your father," Stacey said softly to the little girl as she began to hand her to Ryan.

A piercing shriek rent the air, so completely different from Christy's previous passivity and soft sobs that for a moment Stacey could not believe it was actually the little girl in her arms.

"No! Mommy, Mommy!" the child screamed, clinging tightly to Stacey's neck. "My mommy!"

Chapter Two

Stacey gave Ryan a look of utter bewilderment as the panic-stricken child burrowed her curly head into Stacey's shoulder and clung for dear life. But Ryan's face reflected only the overwhelming relief that he obviously felt at the little girl's safety. Christy's strange reaction was apparently of secondary importance to him.

"It's all right, Christy," Stacey said soothingly, stroking the tiny back. "It's all right." The little body curled so possessively into hers felt wonderfully natural, and for a moment Stacey shut her eyes and silently swayed to comfort the child. Maternal feelings burst through in glorious abandon, and she gave herself up to the delight of the little body so close to her own. But this was not her baby. Another woman should be there to claim this sweet moment. Stacey opened her eyes to stare into Ryan's, which were finally beginning to register an emotion other than relief.

"Is your wife here?" she asked quietly.

"I'm not married."

Stacey's hazel eyes widened in shock, and for an instant the only other emotion she could feel was pure joy like a warm stream surging through her entire body. He wasn't married. Shame followed quickly behind. She was rejoicing because this man had obviously divorced his wife or lost her to death. With Stacey's strongly family background, either eventuality could only be labeled a tragedy. "I'm so sorry," she said, consoling him.

"I'm not," he said with a slow smile.

The sound of more pounding feet preceded the appearance of Caroline, who was running down the path with several other children. The interruption saved Stacey from having to make a response. Ryan knelt to reassure his other daughter of Christy's safety, and Stacey suffered politely the words of praise from Ron and the other guests who had come to help. Sensing her emotional distance, people quickly made discreet exits, and Ron left to tell the searchers at the pond that Christy had been found. Caroline, with a watery smile, gave Stacey and Christy a quick hug before disappearing down the path with the other children. Stacey and Ryan were left alone.

Christy's stiff little body began to relax and Stacey, too discomfited to meet Ryan's gaze, glanced down at the little girl. She was falling asleep, arms still wrapped tightly around Stacey's neck. "I think Christy's completely exhausted," Stacey said, not meeting his eyes. "I'm afraid if I transfer her to you, she'll wake up and start crying again. Do you mind if I take her up to the porch and rock her for a while?"

"Be my guest," he answered. "Both of you could use some rest after what you've been through. I have to say, though, that I envy Christy's position."

Stacey looked at the little girl curled tightly against her breasts. He couldn't mean...

"I'll walk you to the house." With a strong hand under her elbow, Ryan guided her back up the path, their bodies colliding lightly as they stepped over sticks and around rocks. They walked in silence, Stacey too tired and too puzzled to speak, Ryan seemingly too comfortable to need to.

With her fragile burden, Stacey settled herself on the porch swing and, leaning her head back, began to push the ground beneath the swing with her toes. The monotonous motion served to work its magic on her at the same time that she could feel Christy's body slipping deeper into sleep.

Ryan leaned on the front porch railing unabashedly watching the two females on the swing. "You do that very well," he finally said. "As if you've had practice."

She nodded her head and answered softly, "Almost a lifetime of it. Taking care of children is as natural to me as breathing."

"Surely you're too young to have any of your own?"

The words were casual, but they felt like knives hurled at her heart, causing a familiar, aching emptiness. Children of her own; how she wished! "No, not a one," she answered briefly and then changed the subject. "Do you have only the two girls?"

The disarming grin lit his face again, chasing away the shadows that his words has caused for her. "No, actually there is a pair of identical twins, David and Jonathan, who are visiting friends today. Otherwise you wouldn't have failed to notice them. Eight-year-old boys tend to make themselves known."

"Small families are nice," she teased.

"This family is driving me to distraction." His smile took away the sting of the words.

They lapsed into silence again, and Stacey, absolutely aware of his presence, shut her eyes and let the motion of the swing lull her into drowsiness and finally into sleep. In her dream state she felt him approach and stand beside the stationary swing. Almost as if her mind had an eye of its own, she saw him bend over and brush his lips against her forehead. She could smell his clean masculine fragrance and feel the brush of his cheek, slightly rough, against hers. She wanted to reach out to him, to clasp him near and lay her head on the soft mat of hair on his chest. But her arms would not move. Without opening her eyes she knew when he was gone.

Sometime later she felt the small body next to hers begin to stir, and Stacey came instantly awake. "Hello, Christy," she murmured. "How do you feel?"

Instead of the sobs that Stacey expected when the child found herself held by a stranger, the little girl's face lit up in a smile that was a small duplicate of Ryan's.

"Mommy," she said, reaching a tiny hand to pat Stacey's cheek.

"Oh, honey, I'm not your mommy," Stacey said soothingly. "But I sure do love you anyway." The words had slipped out without thought, and Stacey realized that they were true. Even after such a short time, the beautiful little girl felt like her own flesh and blood. Still, she had no business letting the child know her feelings.

"Mommy. My mommy," Christy said, unperturbed by Stacey's words.

"It's time to find Mr. Ryan Cunningham," Stacey said in her best almost-a-schoolteacher voice.

Sounds of merriment were echoing from the vicinity of the barbecue pit, and Stacey and Christy found their way to the picnicking crowd. As if they were visiting royalty, plates of succulent roast pork accompanied by a variety of salads were thrust at them at the same time that room was made for them at one of the picnic tables.

Christy, refusing to leave Stacey's lap even to sit beside her, immediately polished off a major portion of the food on one of the paper plates. Stacey ate as she surveyed the crowd, looking for Ryan, who seemed to have disappeared.

"I hear you were quite the heroine." Margie squeezed in next to them, kissing Christy soundly on the cheek. "By any chance are you looking for someone?"

"I thought Ryan might wonder where Christy was."

"Ryan had to leave. Some kind of trouble with one of the twins. I told him we'd take care of Christy until he could come back and get her. He took Caroline too."

"Well, Christy doesn't seem to mind too much." Stacey inclined her head toward the child, who was now eating Stacey's pork too.

"I'd say she's taken to you," Margie said dryly.

"Feeling's mutual," Stacey murmured, automatically wiping the child's greasy fingers as she finished up the last bit of meat.

"It's my solemn duty to tell you not to get involved in this situation, Stacey. But I have a feeling I'm telling you several hours too late." Margie's tone was serious.

"I'd love to know what situation you're talking about," Stacey answered.

Margie motioned to the little girl. "I'll tell you all about it later." Stacey nodded, indicating agreement that Christy should not be present for the explanation.

But later never arrived. Christy clung, Stacey cajoled, and guests finally began to leave as the hot Florida sun slipped over the horizon in a spectacular sunset.

"I should be going, but I hate to leave Christy until Ryan comes for her," Stacey said, standing next to Margie and waving as the last guest departed.

"Speak of the devil."

A shiny new van rolled up the driveway, barely stopping before children began to spill out of it. Caroline was followed by two dark-haired little boys who faintly resembled Ryan and exactly resembled each other. Stacey watched Ryan swing down from the driver's seat, and her heart lurched against her rib cage. He was still barefooted, even though he had changed into khaki jeans and a brown pullover shirt the color of his curls. Against the backdrop of the spectacular gold and mauve sky, he seemed one with nature. The Tom Sawyer effect was strengthened, and so was the blatant virility. Ryan Cunningham was quite simply a devastating man who would look untamed and rawly powerful in or out of any kind of clothing. The thought, unusual for her in its unabashed sensuality, embarrassed Stacey.

"The sleeping beauties awakened finally." He strode toward them, holding out his arms for Christy. His movements were long and powerful, proclaiming the ease with which his body did his bidding. Unconsciously, Stacey gulped as he came to stand inches from her. "I'm sorry if she's been any trouble," he apologized.

"No trouble at all." But the statement was not true. For Stacey, the trouble was going to start the moment she had to open her arms and give up her claim on the child...and on the child's father.

And Christy, who had seemed happy to see Ryan, began to wail loudly as he pulled her from Stacey. "No, no! Mommy! Mommy!"

"Hush, honey. You have to go now," Stacey crooned, still stroking the child's hair. "Hush now."

"I think I'd better leave quickly," Ryan said to Margie. "Stacey," he said, turning back, "thank you for everything." He bent and brushed a kiss on her cheek before turning to carry the screaming child back to the van. It was a simple kiss, a kiss of gratitude, but it left its mark on Stacey's insides. With a whistle and a shout the other children were collected and piled back into the van. With a roar, which couldn't drown out the still audible screams of the little girl, the van backed down the driveway.

"Want that explanation now?" Margie asked as the last sounds disappeared down the road.

But Stacey was too emotionally overwrought from the wrenching experience of giving up the screaming child to listen to any explanations. "Some other time," she whispered. "I think I'm going to leave now. Please tell everyone good-bye."

With an understanding nod, Margie gave her a quick hug—and a warning. "Just know, honey, that if you get involved with Ryan Cunningham it's going to be like getting involved with a tornado. There is absolutely no guarantee that when he sets you down, no matter how lightly, you'll ever be the same again."

Early the next morning, the dull roar of the room air-conditioner masked the loud banging on Stacey's door. Finally, however, she could no longer ignore the repeated reverberations that threatened to shake the one-room apartment off its concrete block foundations. "I'm coming, hold on."

Swinging her feet over the side of the bed, she finger-combed her hair, which was tumbling around her shoulders in disarray. She pulled on a white cotton robe and padded barefoot to the door, which she unlocked and threw open, covering her yawning mouth with a curled hand.

"Good morning." Ryan, looking haggard and possibly more attractive for it, stood smiling down at her. She had a sudden vision of how she must look herself: haggard and definitely not improved.

"Well, hello," she answered.

"I woke you up."

"I suspect that's plain to see." She motioned him inside.

"You look like a little girl, all flushed and rosy and soft." He stood beside her in the doorway and his hand came up to smooth the hair back from her face. "And your hair looks like rumpled dark sunshine."

"All that and it isn't even eight o'clock yet," she said, aware that her eyes were huge and probably revealing the internal trembling his words had caused. She pulled away from the magic of his hand resting lightly on her hair. "May I make you some coffee?"

"No, but you can come home with me."

It was too much. She sank onto the sofa bed, glad for once that her apartment was so small that there was furniture everywhere. "I can't come home with you, Ryan. Whatever do you want me for?"

The haggard expression lifted as he threw back his head and laughed. Haggard, he was gorgeous; laughing, he was.... She shut her eyes as no words superlative enough reached her foggy brain.

"If you have no idea what a red-blooded man would want you for, Georgia Brown, then you are just as innocent as you look." He laughed again as her eyes snapped open. "But in this case, I need you to come home with me to try and comfort Christy. She's been screaming since I pulled her away from you last night. I'm afraid she's going to be very sick if this keeps up." There was no laughter left in his eyes, only concern.

Stacey whistled softly. "I'm so sorry to hear that," she said. "Of course, I'll come; just wait till I get some clothes on."

"If I have to," he said with a glint of humor.

Ignoring his innuendos, she gathered up coral shorts and a matching halter and hurried into the bathroom to change. Her own sleepless night stared back at her from the mirror, but she ignored the circles under her eyes, only stopping long enough to run a comb through her tumbled hair and to brush her teeth. "Let's go," she said as she emerged.

"Stacey, you're like a breath of fresh air," Ryan said with real gratitude. "Every other woman I know would have taken an hour to get ready."

She couldn't resist. "Then obviously you know the wrong women," she said sweetly.

The van was double-parked outside, and Stacey murmured apologies to her neighbor who, because of the van, had been unable to pull his car out. In a minute she and Ryan were tearing down the quiet street.

When the pace slowed, she turned covertly and watched him bend over the wheel. The van interior was like a small traveling palace; they were encased in deep blue velour seats and surrounded by rich, dark paneling. "You know," she said finally, "if I'm going to deal with this situation constructively, at least I ought to know what's going on."

Ryan glanced sideways in surprise. "I'm sorry. What is it that you don't know?"

"How can I tell you if I don't know what I don't know?"

"Try telling me what you do know."

Frustration of this magnitude was not easy to cope with. She tried again. "You are Ryan Cunningham, world-famous architect. You have four lovely children and no wife, which doesn't seem to bother you in the least bit. Doesn't that seem strange to you at all, or am I so archaic that single parenthood of that proportion only seems odd to me?"

Concern for Christy did not seem to have dimmed his sense of humor even a little bit. When the laughter died he grew serious only gradually. "I thought you knew the story. Of course you're confused. It's simple. The children aren't mine."

"That's simple?" Stacey could think of nothing else to say.

"Well, actually, they are mine now." He was silent for a moment and Stacey, completely disoriented, sat quietly watching him. Finally he began again. "The children are my nieces and nephews. Their mother and father were killed in a plane crash six months ago."

"Oh, Ryan!" She was instantly contrite for her impatience with him. "How terrible for all of you."

"I was staying with the children so that my sister Janelle and her husband Tom could have a second honeymoon. I wanted to get to know the kids better, and I knew Janelle and Tom needed some time alone. They were killed along with the pilot, flying back home in my plane. Lending it to them was part of my gift,'' he said bitterly.

"How responsible you must have felt,'' she said with sympathy.

Ryan took his eyes off the road long enough to shoot her a penetrating look. "No one else has ever understood that,'' he said.

"Sometimes people forget how easy it is to fall prey to natural feelings like guilt when you're in pain.'' She watched the van hug the side of the road as it slowed down to take a curve. Finally she went on: "And the children remained with you?''

"I was granted temporary custody. But the children will remain with me always,'' he added with a note of steel in his voice.

"It hasn't been easy, I'm sure. That explains why Christy seems so depressed.''

"It's been terribly hard for all the kids. The twins fight all the time; Caroline tries to mother everybody; and Christy cries. But Christy has made the worst adjustment. She was a bright, happy little girl until this happened. Now she hardly eats, and she's almost quit talking.''

"She ate enough last night at the party to last her for a week,'' Stacey said, consoling him.

Ryan favored her with a warm smile that sent her head reeling. "That was your doing. She's completely taken with you.''

"Am I anything like her mother, Ryan?''

"In looks? No, not at all. Janelle was small too, but much more fragile than you are. And she had dark, curly hair like mine and lots of freckles. No, you don't look like Janelle, but you're sweet and caring like she was, and

I'm sure Christy senses that. Christy is desperate for a mother."

"What a mess," Stacey murmured sadly. "I'd love to help out, but I'm afraid that she'll see the time I can't spend with her as a rejection. She needs a full-time, permanent mother, not a sometimes substitute."

"Let's just see what happens," he said mysteriously.

They pulled up in front of a modern condominium complex of sleek gray concrete and angles accented by exotic plantings of native shrubbery. Through a covered walkway Stacey could see an Olympic-sized outdoor pool surrounded by the tanned, shining bodies of young, athletic women and men. There was no playground; there were no children in sight.

Ryan saw the disapproval that she didn't take the trouble to hide as he came around to escort her to a doorway. "I know. It's exactly the wrong kind of place for them to be. Wait until you see the inside; it's just as bad."

He was wrong. Inside was much, much worse. The entryway to the small apartment was papered in delicate white rice paper decorated now with children's handprints. The carpet, a pastel silvery blue, looked as though it would only tolerate bare feet or slippers. It had not tolerated the galloping, muddy shoes of four pairs of young feet. Ground-in dirt shone through the fibers like a billboard advertising the fact that children lived there.

They were greeted by an old woman would could only be described as frantic. "Mr. Cunningham, I can't do a thing with this child," she said in a voice that portended the beginnings of a stress-related heart attack. In her arms was a wailing Christy.

"Come here, baby," Stacey said without thinking. "Come here, Christy." With a sob and a hiccup, Christy launched herself into Stacey's arms and wound her arms around her neck.

"Mommy!"

It seemed the height of cruelty to correct her, and Stacey stoically ignored her new title. "I'm here, honey. I know it will take a while, but I want you to try and stop crying." She held the little girl tightly against her as she followed Ryan into the living room.

It was a small room, furnished in sleekly contemporary furniture that looked cold and remarkably fragile: glass-topped tables; wooden chairs that looked like thin, twisted sticks held together by paste and by prayer; and gleaming metal lamps that were all exposed light bulb and delicate globe. "Whew," she exclaimed over Christy's hiccups. "My younger brothers could destroy this entire room in five minutes without even trying."

As if on cue, two dark heads appeared around the corner. "It's my Walkman, not yours. Give it here before I bust you one." With a graceful movement that looked surprisingly like a karate exercise, Ryan captured a small boy in each hand.

"Going somewhere?" he questioned them.

"He took my..."

"No, he did!"

With a resoluteness that would have done a much more experienced father proud, Ryan took care of the situation and then brought the boys to meet Stacey. "Boys, meet Stacey MacDonald, a friend of mine."

"Another friend? You sure do have lots of girl friends," said the boy identified as David.

"Yeah, you sure do," Jonathan added, united with his brother now to get even with their uncle.

Stacey, unperturbed by their rudeness, smiled at the childish maneuvers. "Hello, Jonathan, David. I'm glad to meet you both."

Caroline wandered into the room, followed by the old woman, who was introduced as Mrs. Watson, Ryan's long-time housekeeper. The room, small at best, was now completely full.

"Uh, sit down, Stacey. Mrs. Watson is fixing breakfast for us."

"One egg or two, miss?" Mrs. Watson was favoring Stacey with a smile of such overwhelming gratitude that Stacey could hardly keep a straight face. "Oh, two, thanks."

Stacey turned to Ryan, who was appreciatively eyeing her soft, generous curves. "I like a woman who eats," he murmured with a smile.

"I was taught that was what food was for," she said with a noticeable drawl. Back to Scarlett O'Hara, she realized with dismay.

Breakfast was a repeat of dinner the night before; Christy sat on Stacey's lap and ate everything in sight. Evidently a night of misery was good for the appetite. Stacey set out to win the hearts of the two boys and engaged them in intricate conversation about the relative merits of different space movies. By the end of the raucous meal, she had won their approval—chiefly, she decided, because she had never once referred to them as the twins or expected them to think or act alike. Caroline visibly relaxed as the meal progressed without the tensions of fighting or of Christy's crying.

Stacey regarded the older girl with a stab of pity. It was apparent that Caroline felt responsibility for keeping her family happy and together. She was growing up much too fast; losing her parents was enough to cope with by itself. Resolving to talk to Ryan about getting some more help with the children, Stacey looked directly at him for the first time since she had sat down at the crowded table. He was watching her with the disarming grin that she had found so enchanting the day before, and her heart did a repeat flip-flop. Watch out, she cautioned herself. This one was entirely too dangerous, even unmarried.

"Get your suits on, kids, and Mrs. Watson will watch you swim for a while," Ryan announced after breakfast.

With a series of mumbles and groans the children, except Christy, raced into the other room to change. "Do children always grumble, even if they want to do something?" he asked Stacey.

"Always." She smiled and offered him badly needed encouragement. "You're doing a very good job with them, Ryan. You handle David and Jonathan like a pro. And it's not your fault that Christy needs a mother."

He shrugged. "I know I'm doing what I can. But it's not enough." His face lit up and he reached out to cover her hand, perched on her coffee cup, with his. "And that's where you come in."

She relished the feel of his large, strong hand covering her delicate one as she looked up at him to search his face. "Me?"

"Margie tells me you need a summer job."

"When did you talk to Margie?" she asked in confusion.

"This morning, when I called her for your address."

She blinked. "Frankly, I'm surprised that she gave it to you."

"I had to swear on a stack of apple pies that I'd treat you with the respect and good taste you deserved, and then I had to listen to a lecture on how to treat a lady, before she gave it to me."

"Believe me," Stacey said, laughing, "you got off easy. Obviously she trusts you."

"If she does, she's crazy," he said, giving her another appreciative appraisal. "But she did say that you didn't have plans for the summer."

"And?"

"And I have a proposition to make you," he continued.

"Not in front of Christy," Stacey warned him with a twinkle.

"I want you to move in with me. Starting today."

She bent over, her dark honey hair falling like a veil between them as she pretended to wipe Christy's mouth with her napkin. "Well," she said, as she finally felt courageous enough to answer him, "that's quite a proposition."

"Care to hear the whole thing?" he asked, obviously amused at her reaction.

"I can't wait," she said faintly.

Ryan rose and helped her out of her chair. She followed him into the living room and took a place on the sofa where she and Christy could stretch out a little. To her surprise, he sat next to them, his larger body radiating warmth and something more.

"I want to take the children camping for a month in the mountains of western North Carolina," he began. "This place is completely inappropriate for them, and besides it's against the rules to have children here. The people who manage the condominiums have been understanding, but they're not going to be patient forever."

"What are you going to do about a place to live after the month is up?" she queried.

"I've purchased fifty acres and a house near where Ron and Margie live. The house is very old and needs a lot of renovating before it'll be livable. I've got a crew going full steam ahead on it right now, but it won't be ready for at least another six weeks."

"It sounds perfect for the children," Stacey mused.

"It will be. But in the meantime, I want to get them out of here, and I want to keep them busy. A camping trip seems like the perfect solution. By the time we get back, the house will be almost finished."

"And where do I come in?"

Ryan turned to smile fully at her. "You'll come camping too. I don't think, truthfully, that I can handle this whole bunch by myself for a month in the wilderness; I might be tempted to leave some of them for the bears. I'm going to need help."

Stacey thought about his words. Somehow she would have pictured Ryan Cunningham, world-famed architect, on a far-off exotic shore at a luau or curled up with a beautiful model in front of the fire at a snowy ski lodge. Was this the same man whom she had tagged in her memory as living in the fast lane? This man who wanted only to take four parentless children on a camping trip to a local mountain range? And where would she fit in? For Pete's sake, where would she sleep?

"This is a bit out of the ordinary, Ryan," she stammered. "I think it's going to look a bit, ummm...shady if I go off on a month-long camping trip with you, much less live here before we go."

"Shady?" He threw back his head and she could see shudders of laughter rippling through his husky frame. "Are you worried about your reputation, Georgia peach?"

Stacey bristled. "Maybe that's not important to you, but it is to me."

"Why, you are serious, aren't you?" He sobered slowly. "Haven't you ever read any nineteenth-century gothic novels? Just tell your friends that you've been hired as a governess," he said, cajoling her, an affectionate light in his brown eyes.

"A governess in a tent?"

"Stacey, Stacey, no matter how much I might want to fool around with you, what could I do with four children watching us? You'll be perfectly safe. And you and the girls can sleep in a tent by yourselves. Your virtue will be intact."

He was making sense, although she had a definite feeling of disappointment at his words. It would have been nice at least to have suspicions that he had some amount of hanky-panky on his mind. With a sigh, she said, hedging, "Surely there's someone you know better and are closer to that you can invite."

"Everyone I know well enough is inappropriate," he said shortly. "Stacey, you're the only woman I know who will do. You can name your price."

A few minutes later, as she laid a sleeping Christy in her crib in the cramped bedroom, with Christy still holding firmly to her hand, she knew that the ultimate price was the happiness of one little girl. With her best instincts screaming at her to run out the door and never look back, Stacey told a grateful Ryan that she would spend her summer with him. And when he pulled her close and placed a slow, not-quite-brotherly kiss on her cheek, she knew instinctively that her life would never be the same again.

Chapter Three

"Let's try it one more time, kids," Stacey wheedled as the tent, resplendent in its green and white glory, sank majestically to the ground in front of Ryan's condominium, a spreading pool of mosquito netting and canvas. "Just one more time."

"Did you try reading the directions?" Ryan's teasing voice sounded behind her, and Stacey turned with a whirl of pigtails and an accusing expression on her face. "Several times, Mr. Cunningham. You try it if you think you know so much."

"I used to go camping all the time when Janelle and I were kids. Watch a master do it." Rolling up the sleeves of his white dress shirt and loosening his tie, Ryan conferred with the children, assigning jobs to each of them. Even Christy was recruited to pound stakes into the ground with a wooden hammer.

The tent went up like magic. "Is it safe to go inside now"?" David asked doubtfully. "Last time I did, it fell on my head."

"Go ahead, honey," Stacey said with a red face. "I think it's finally up."

"Nice job, wouldn't you say, Stacey?" Ryan teased as he pulled his shirt sleeves down over the strong sinews of his forearms.

"I've been taught always to tell the truth, but boy, it sure grates sometimes," she answered with a flick of her pigtails. "All right, you did a nice job. Satisfied?"

Ryan laid a companionable arm on her shoulder and looked down at the pigtails topping off an outfit of white cut-offs, yellow T-shirt and bare feet. "You know, Stacey, you won't have to worry about your reputation on this trip at all. If you dress like this, everyone will think you're my kid too."

"Just as long as you act as though I were, we'll get along fine," she blurted without thinking.

Ryan's body next to hers was shaking with silent laughter, and his arm tightened around her shoulder. From experience now, she recognized the familiar sensation of heat surging through her body at his touch. "Sweet Georgia gal, your virtue is safe with me."

Pulling away, she faced him, hands on her curving hips. "Have you bought a tent for you and the boys yet?"

"Better than that. My parents packed up the one I used to use as a kid and mailed it to me. The package just came." This was a side of Ryan that still amazed her, even after being in almost constant contact with him for two weeks. The man who seemed free and easy on the surface, and whose architecture reflected the most progressive trends of the twentieth century, was really a traditionalist at heart. It was just like him to want to sleep in the tent he had loved as a boy. This surprising sentimentality sent a warm glow of affection coursing through her body. It explained why he would renovate an old farmhouse instead of building something of his own design, and it explained why he was trying to become the father of four rambunctious children. Ryan Cunningham was a very special man.

"Are you sure the tent's in good shape after all those years?" She emphasized the last three words.

"They don't make them like they used to. That tent will last a century." He reached out and pulled a silky pigtail. "And don't you get too sassy. Don't forget, starting tomorrow you're going to be at my mercy for a whole month."

The two weeks since Stacey had made the summer commitment to Ryan had slipped by in a flurry of hours spent trying to organize the children and the proposed camping trip. The only change in plan that Stacey had insisted on was her refusal to live in the condominium before the trip. Instead she had moved Christy and Caroline to her own apartment at night, a move that had served to establish a warm rapport between herself and the older girl while meeting Christy's needs for a nurturing relationship. Daytime had been spent buying camping equipment and appropriate clothing for everyone.

"I hope we're prepared," Stacey mused as she and Ryan supervised the kids, who were taking the tent down again and preparing it for packing. "I've tried to think of everything."

"That reminds me, I looked at the stove you suggested we buy and decided to do without one. I want this to be a real back-to-nature experience for the kids, so I think we'll cook over an open fire." Ryan bent to pull out one forgotten stake.

Sentimentality was fine—up to a point. "I hope you're planning on doing the cooking then," Stacey trilled sweetly.

"Only if you put up the tents," he answered, his torso still upside down, "and chop the firewood, and dig the trenches, and..."

The next day dawned with the hot sweetness of a July Florida morning. Stacey awoke earlier than the two little girls sleeping beside her, and she stretched carefully so as not to awaken them. Pillowing her head on her hands, she gave in to the excitement building from her toes to the top of her dark golden hair. In less than an hour Ryan would arrive to pack the few belongings that were at her apartment, and the trip would begin.

Stacey had never been on a vacation before, although she would no more have admitted that fact to anyone than she would have strolled naked down West Tennessee Street. The prospect of an entire month spent on something so frivolous was completely foreign and delicious. And spending an entire month with Ryan Cunningham was even more intriguing.

Ryan Cunningham. Just the name was enough these days to send spiraling sensations of pleasure through her body. Ryan Cunningham with the dark, dancing eyes and the raw-boned, daredevil face. Ryan Cunningham, whose presence in the room could turn her insides into a facsimile of Grandma's homemade blackberry jelly. Her attraction to him, with its beginnings rooted in the first moment she had seen him standing in Margie's doorway, had grown and was growing still. Ryan Cunningham had grown into her heart.

And why this particular man, she asked herself, as she lay quietly watching the two little girls beside her? How much of her fascination was for his children and their cherub attractions?

But try as she might to rationalize her feelings, the truth was that the love she had developed for the children was a separate entity. When she thought of Ryan, it was not with four little bodies in the picture. It was of him, by himself, caressing her with his eyes and with his fine, strong hands.

In the last weeks, however, Ryan's hands had stayed firmly where they belonged. If indeed he sometimes looked at her in a way that sent sparks flying between them, there had been no other signs of a desire for greater intimacy. Instead, Stacey was aware that Ryan was spending time with other women. He didn't flaunt it, but he didn't hide the fact either. Fatherhood with all its demands did not seem to have dimmed his social life. Margie, with her concerns about Stacey's purity, would have been pleased. Stacey was devastated.

"Is it time to get up?" Caroline sat up in bed rubbing her eyes. The day had started, and within minutes the three females were up, dressed, and waiting impatiently for Ryan.

Excitement was at a fever pitch when the dark blue van pulled up in Stacey's driveway. With a minimum of effort, luggage was loaded, and everyone settled into the places that Stacey had so carefully diagrammed. "Jonathan, you get the captain's chair behind Uncle Ryan for the first hour. David, you get the sofa next to Christy."

Ryan cut loose with an appreciative whistle. "You have a career as a drill sergeant awaiting you."

Stacey, sitting in the front, appraised him as they pulled out onto the highway. Dressed in an olive Hawaiian print shirt and brown shorts, he was barefoot as usual. She had discovered quickly that Ryan wore shoes only when he had to. The patterned shirt was unbuttoned halfway down his chest, revealing more tanned skin and curling hair than was safe for her to see. "You look pretty good yourself," he said with a smile in response to her scrutiny.

Stacey, who had taken more time than usual picking out her clothes, was glad that he had noticed. The terry cloth playsuit of soft oatmeal and turquoise was one of her favorites. Pinning up her hair in a loose knot on top of her head, she had achieved the effect that she wanted. Casual, summery, and worth looking at twice. And the playsuit was just tight enough in the right places to assure any onlookers that she was most certainly not one of Ryan's kids.

They drove north to Georgia through gently rolling countryside punctuated by unpainted wooden houses graced with rusting tin roofs and rickety front porches. The children clamored to stop and buy watermelon from a sleeping man under a canopy who had dozens of huge melons and a For Sale sign to keep him company. They passed on, Ryan insisting that it was too early to take a break.

Tiny towns with one stop light flashed by. Red clay, scrubby pines, and pecan orchards behind wooden fences marked their entry into real Georgia farmland. By the time they were ready to stop for lunch they were in Cordele, watermelon capital of the world. Ryan was persuaded to visit the sprawling farmers' market and pick out a juicy, ripe melon from a farmer who gave free samples to the children. Apparently charmed by their excitement, the old man charged them one dollar and refused to take more.

Tired of traveling and satiated by a lunch of fast food pleasures, all four children curled up and slept through the next portion of the trip. Stacey was fascinated by the big-leafed kudzu vines making soft sculptures of the trees and shrubs that they were slowly overtaking.

"That's an eerie sight, isn't it?" she mused out loud. "So soft and inviting. The vines hide everything, making you forget that a whole forest is dying beneath it. Meanwhile, the kudzu continues to rampage through the countryside devouring everything in sight."

"Sort of like some women I've known," Ryan observed.

His words were humorously sarcastic, not bitter, and Stacey thought about them before answering. "Why would you persist in knowing women like that?" she asked.

"Probably so I'd have an excuse not to settle down. If I make an effort not to find the right woman, then I can stay as free as that hawk circling overhead."

She realized that he wasn't teasing her; he was perfectly serious. "And freedom is that important?"

"It always seemed to be. Now I'm not so sure. I'm about as tied down as a man can get, and I wouldn't trade places with anyone anywhere."

"I had to sing a song once for a talent show. One of the lines was 'Freedom's just another word for nothing left to lose.'" She stopped quoting. "I guess I was brought up to believe that's true."

"It shows, Stacey. It shows." His voice was a surprising caress. "Tell me about that talent show. What was it like to almost be Miss Georgia?"

Margie had been at work again, although why she had felt Ryan needed that piece of information would probably always remain her secret. Stacey thought about his question. "It was terrifying and exciting and embarrassing, probably in that order. I was only nineteen when I entered the local pageant. They were offering small scholarships to the first three finalists, and I needed the money desperately. No one was more surprised than I when I won, but then the whole thing snowballed."

"How so?" She was grateful to hear no trace of amusement in his voice.

"Well, practically the next thing I knew I was a celebrity. People were taking my picture every minute, teaching me how to walk, how to dress, how to fix my hair and my makeup. Suddenly I was being given singing lessons and speaking lessons. One minute I was a simple Georgia farm girl and the next minute the entire town of Gainesville had their hopes pinned on me."

"So what did you do?"

"Do? I couldn't do a thing. I was on a train bound for glory and I couldn't get off. It was completely out of my control." She stopped and drew a deep breath. "By the time the big pageant began, I felt like a facsimile of myself. The real Stacey MacDonald would never have gotten up on that huge stage and pranced around in a bathing suit and evening gown. The real Stacey MacDonald would never have gotten up in front of all those people and sung a medley of Broadway songs that she had practically never heard before. When they announced that I was the first runner-up, I cried, but they were tears of sheer joy."

"Joy?"

"I'd have lost myself forever if I had won. Knowing it was over was the greatest moment of my life."

Ryan was completely silent and the miles ticked by as they both stared out at the road. Finally he responded. "Georgia gal, you're one of a kind. You almost restore my faith in human beings."

For now, she decided, "almost" would have to do.

The children woke up one at a time, grumpy and fretful. Stacey was kept busy entertaining them as Ryan drove. Rest breaks became more and more frequent until finally, outside the far-reaching suburbs of Atlanta, they stopped in exhaustion.

"I really thought we'd make it to the mountains tonight," Ryan said in disgust. "It's hardly worth camping just for one night, but if I suggest a motel the kids will murder me."

After a quick consultation with the camping guide, Ryan got back on the interstate highway, and an hour later they pulled in under a wooden sign. "Kamper's Kingdom," it proclaimed.

"Are you sure this isn't a drive-in movie?" Stacey asked as she viewed the narrow, regimented camping spaces.

Shooting her a look that would have silenced an auditorium full of giggling teenage girls, Ryan turned to the kids. "We're here; everybody out."

It was twilight, which hardly seemed to matter, since the entire campground was illuminated by huge search-lights that would have done a prison compound proud. The only camping spot that was left was a site composed of tiny rocks, perfect for a trailer and miserable for a tent. After careful consideration, Ryan announced that he and the boys would sleep out under the stars without benefit of cover. The tent was just too much trouble to set up for one night. Stacey and the girls would sleep in the van.

"Are you sure, Ryan? What if it rains?"

"There's not a cloud in the sky, Stacey. Stop worrying."

At Stacey's insistence they had eaten before finding the campground, so after their meager set-up preparations were completed, they crossed the lot to the dressing rooms and changed into swim suits. Ryan's eyes passed over Stacey's lush curves under the ivory maillot bathing suit, sending pleasure prickles up her spine. "Very nice," he said softly. "You would have had my vote."

The pool, already crowded with squirming bodies, was shallow and tepid. Christy clung to Stacey in intelligent fear of drowning, but there was no reason to be afraid. With so many people in the pool, there was almost no water available to drown in. Halfheartedly they splashed for a few minutes and then, wrapped in fluffy beach towels, picked their way carefully across the crowded sites back to the van.

"Well, we can't have a campfire to roast marshmal-lows tonight," Stacey said, thinking out loud. Their campsite boasted only one small barbecue grill large enough for half a dozen charcoal briquettes. "I think a sing-along is out of the question too." The noise of a dozen TV sets and radios, all tuned to different stations, sounded merrily throughout the campground. There seemed to be nothing left to do except pile into the van and tell ghost stories.

Even inside the van with the curtains drawn, it was barely dark enough to set a proper atmosphere. Ryan and Caroline curled up on the rug at the foot of the comfortable sofa bed in the back of the van. Stacey and the boys, with Christy sandwiched between them, sat on the sofa. With hardly room to move, Stacey was very conscious of her long expanse of bare leg rubbing sensuously against Ryan's cheek.

The ghost stories began with the boys telling tales that they had learned at a slumber party the previous year. Next, Caroline innocently told a story that left Ryan and Stacey with their mouths hanging open. The double meanings, hopefully over the children's head, were quite clear to the two adults, and Stacey was blushing.

"My turn," she said quickly, hoping to subvert any further offerings that Caroline might have. "Once upon a time an old woman lived all alone in an apartment on top of a skyscraper in a big city." Stoically she ignored Ryan's moans. The story continued, suspense building as Stacey told of the repeated frightening phone calls the old woman received. Her voice got lower and lower as she repeated the message, "I'm the viper, and I'm coming..."

The children huddled closer and Stacey, delighted by her rapport with the audience, got more and more dramatic. Not since that night she had almost gotten the title that she didn't want had she held so many people in the palm of her hand. Suddenly, without warning, into the hushed atmosphere came an explosive *zing* that sent Stacey careening off the sofa straight into Ryan's arms.

"What on earth—" she managed to gasp out as she extracted herself in mortification from his hard, bare chest, peeling four little bodies off him at the same time.

"It's the viper," Ryan hissed menacingly. "It's Max the Viper. He's coming to 'vipe your vindows.'"

"You beast," she cried, pummeling him fiercely. "You gave it away. You must have gone to the same girl scout camp I did." Another *zing* sent her into his arms again, this time for keeps.

"I'm not letting go of you any more, Georgia gal. Not until I'm sure you won't bowl me over again." With strong arms around her waist, he settled her comfortably on his lap. His breath was warm on her cheek and she could smell the faint, pleasant odor of pool chlorine on his skin, mixed with his own clean scent. She was keenly aware that the only clothing separating them were two fairly skimpy bathing suits, and she luxuriated in the feel of his warm body against hers.

"It's a bug zapper," Caroline announced with enthusiasm as she courageously peered out of the van. "The people next door set up the biggest bug zapper I've ever seen and it zings every time it kills a bug."

"Oh, great," Stacey said in disgust, relaxing for a moment against Ryan. "So much for the great American wilderness experience."

The children all scurried out of the van to investigate this newest attraction. "By tomorrow morning, there will be hundreds of slimy, warty toads crowded under that thing eating dead bugs," Ryan intoned, his chin resting on Stacey's head.

"Well, wildlife is what we were after," she drawled, her voice sounding peculiarly as if it belonged exclusively in Georgia. All this man had to do was touch her and she lost whatever cosmopolitan veneer she had managed to acquire.

"Your hair smells like sunlight and honeysuckle," Ryan added softly as the children filed back into the van. "And if your cousin could see us now, she'd be fit to be tied." With what sounded like a sigh, he unwrapped his arms, freeing Stacey from his warm embrace. "I think it's time for bed."

With ceremonial reverence, the boys unrolled their sleeping bags and pumped up their air mattresses. Ryan, disdaining such luxuries, threw his old, worn sleeping bag directly on the pebbles next to the van. Stacey and the girls pulled the curtains, changed into T-shirts and shorts for sleeping, and then made the careful trek across camp to the bathroom where they waited in line to brush their teeth.

With a minimum of giggling, the tired children settled in to sleep for the duration. But even if the campground had been as quiet as a wilderness night, Stacey would not have been able to fall asleep quickly. As it was, with televisions and radios blaring and bug zappers zinging, it was well into morning before she slept. Somewhere between the time that the people in the trailers next door turned on its noisy air-conditioner and the poodle in the camper on the other side began to howl, she finally drifted off.

And sometime soon after that, dew like a heavy, wet blanket settled over the campground, soaking everything in sight...including one grown man and two little boys. With childish good sense, the boys were the first to react. David, damp and chilled, woke Stacey up when he slid open the side door of the van, but before he could close it, Jonathan was at his side. Stacey found beach towels and dried them each off as best she could, tucking them into bed beside their sleeping sisters. Their combined body heat warmed them up quickly and they fell asleep again in moments.

Luckily the captain's chairs reclined, and with a thankful prayer for Ryan's foresight, Stacey snapped one of the chairs back and curled up under an extra blanket to go back to sleep. As her eyes were closing, she stole a glance out of the window at Ryan's sleeping form. Tom Sawyer could not have been any wetter if he had been dumped off his raft in the middle of the mighty Mississippi.

With a martyr's sigh, Stacey got up, threw off her blanket, and slid the van door open once again. Kneeling beside Ryan, she shook him gently. "Ryan, wake up. You're soaked." Not only was he covered with dew, but the moisture from the ground beneath him, with no air mattress to block it, was seeping into his sleeping bag.

"Ryan," she said more loudly.

"Shhhh...decent people are trying to sleep," said a prim old-lady voice from the poodle's camper.

Gritting her teeth, Stacey shook Ryan again. "Ryan," she whispered in his ear, "wake up!"

Strong arms came around her suddenly, pulling her down on top of his long body. "I was just dreaming about you," his voice, husky from sleep, growled in her ear. "I dreamed we were walking in the rain."

Her heart was pounding as if it wanted to escape from her rib cage. Even with a sleeping bag separating them the experience of her body fully on top of his was soul-scorching. "You're dreaming about the rain because you're soaking wet," she admonished in a voice that didn't sound stern at all.

"I'm also cold," he admitted. "Come in here and warm me up." He fumbled around for the zipper.

"Ryan, I can't!" she cried, more loudly than she had intended.

"If you two don't stop that obscene behavior, I'm going to get the camp manager," screeched the old lady in the camper.

Ryan's eyes were blazing. "Lady, take your poodle and your bug zapper and..."

Using desperate measures, Stacey silenced his profanity with a kiss. Ryan's mouth beneath hers was wet and warm, and his taste was as delicious as she knew it would be. Forgetting the old lady for a moment, Stacey gave herself completely to her chosen task of keeping him quiet. Too soon she realized that she had succeeded beyond her wildest expectations. He was kissing her back with obvious enjoyment.

At the point where his tongue began to investigate the feather-soft inside of her bottom lip, she realized that her Good Samaritan gesture had gotten completely out of hand. Pulling away, she jumped to her feet in consternation. "Well, I'm not going to stay out here and freeze to death," she said haughtily. Ryan's laughter echoed after her as she swept back into the van.

To her ultimate satisfaction, Ryan followed her inside a few minutes later. Silently she tossed him a towel before she settled down once again to go to sleep. The creak of the other captain's chair as it was moved into its reclining position and the rustle of blankets were almost the last sounds she heard. As her eyelashes touched her cheeks, she heard him whisper, "Good night, Georgia peach."

Chapter Four

The arrival of the sun the next morning was inconspicuous. Kamper's Kingdom had neglected to turn off its giant searchlights, and the campground had remained as brightly lit throughout the night as Waikiki at midday. The four children were not fooled, however, and at their usual early hour they were swarming all over Stacey and Ryan.

Stacey discovered something about Ryan that she had not had occasion to know before; he was not a cheerful person in the morning. With little more than a grunt and a mumble he stuffed sleeping bags under seats while Stacey shepherded the children to the safety of the camp bathrooms. After faces were scrubbed and hair tangles were smoothed out, they were unceremoniously packed into the van to finish the trip to North Carolina.

"Generally, the practice of eating breakfast has sound merit," she mentioned, tongue in cheek, to Ryan as they pulled out of the campground. His dark curls were hanging over his forehead in disarray and his sleep-flushed cheeks and night's growth of beard made him look like a rakish detective in a television series.

"I never eat breakfast." he said shortly.

"But your children do."

"Can't we train them otherwise?" he asked with a ghost of a grin.

"When they're about twenty-one, maybe." Stacey watched the scenery flick by until they slowed down to pull into a truck stop advertising home-cooked meals.

As if it were a magic potion, Stacey watched Ryan's attitude change with each swallow of the black coffee he ordered. The children at a booth by themselves gobbled up platters of ham and eggs, grits drenched with melted butter, and fresh country biscuits with honey. Christy couldn't seem to get enough to eat, consuming her weight in biscuits alone.

"She's doing so much better," Ryan observed, growing more cheerful as he cut a biscuit open and stuffed it with a piece of ham. "It's hard to believe she's the same child."

Christy was doing better. Although she still clung to Stacey, she was beginning to venture out into the world again. In the short weeks since Stacey had taken over her care, she had seen a vast improvement in the little girl's speech. New words were cropping up all the time and she was beginning to speak in sentences. It would take a little while, but Christy would be fine.

The other children were showing a good surface adjustment. The twins seemed to have coped with the tragedy more easily than the two girls. With the special bonding that only twins can understand, they had managed to help each other through their sadness. If at times they still lashed out in pain, they also offered comfort and understanding in a way that was reassuring to see.

Caroline was the one who worried Stacey. Although she seemed to be in perfect control of her emotions, there was a haunted look about her that wrenched Stacey's heart. That Caroline was still suffering was evident in the way she refused to talk about her feelings. As far as the young girl was concerned, the subject of her parents was closed. She would not respond to any discussion of them, changing the subject instantly if they were brought up. It was almost as if the pain inside was still so overwhelming that bringing it out in the open would drown her in its agony.

Stacey and Ryan had discussed the problem briefly and decided that only patience and time could provide the answers that Caroline needed. In the meantime, they continued to wait for her to begin expressing her inner turmoil. By taking the burden of Christy off the girl's fragile shoulders, Stacey hoped that she was giving her room to deal with her own emotions.

"They're such beautiful children," Stacey said to Ryan in a burst of enthusiasm. She knew better than to blurt out her feelings, but sometimes she was overwhelmed by them. "I'm falling in love." She took a sip of her coffee and settled back in the red vinyl booth. When she looked at Ryan he was watching her closely, his straight, thick eyebrows knit in a frown, his mahogany curls resting in the furrow of his forehead.

"You know, the only problem with this arrangement is that when you leave, the children will feel as if they've lost another parent," he said quietly.

It was true, and it worried her. She took another sip of coffee. "I think I have a solution of sorts."

"What's that?"

"I'd like to have your permission to continue to spend some time with them after the summer has ended. I know eventually they'll forget about me, but staying in touch for a while might help ease their sense of loss." She finished with a sigh and glumly examined the coffee grounds in her now empty cup.

"What about your sense of loss, Georgia Brown?"

He was right. Here it was only July, the beginning of their time together, and already she was worried about leaving them. All of them. There was no point in hiding her feelings. Looking straight into his eyes she answered, "I'm going to miss them a lot, Ryan. I keep thinking I ought to hold back a little for everybody's sake, but I just can't. As long as I'm with them, I'm just going to have to take a chance that the love I feel isn't going to damage any of us too badly."

Ryan seemed amazed at her candor, and for a long moment their eyes held. The indefinable sparks that sometimes flew between them almost ignited the paper napkins on the table. It was too much for Stacey. She excused herself to go check on Christy, who was trying to jump out of her high chair. When Stacey finally slid into her seat again the spell had been broken.

They finished breakfast, taking some extra biscuits and ham for a picnic lunch. Then they were buckling seat belts and preparing for the trip to North Carolina. After an hour on the road, Stacey pointed to a turnoff. "That's the way to my parents' house."

"We were that close and you didn't tell me last night?" Ryan teased, his eyes turning casually to the exit. "We could have descended on them."

"To be honest, I haven't told my parents about this trip," she said apologetically. "And I've sworn Margie to secrecy. I may be twenty-three, but if my parents found out that I was camping with a man, no matter what the circumstances, I think they'd still take me out behind the woodshed and apply the old willow switch."

Ryan flashed her a heartbreaking grin. No one, she decided, looked like Ryan when he grinned. Mischievous and charming little boy poured out like liquid sunshine. But the analogy wasn't quite correct, because everything about Ryan was overwhelmingly grown-up male.

His eyes had flickered to her bottom, encased in brief denim cut-offs, as if he was imagining the sight of her turned over someone's knee. "And well they should!" He pretended to be stern. "Whoever heard of such a thing?"

"Certainly nobody in my family, that's for sure. They're still talking about the time three years ago when my oldest brother eloped with a girl down the road. Greg and Sue don't have any children, but when they do, everybody will say: 'See, what did I tell you? I knew they had to get married!'"

There was another grin. "So that's what it's like to grow up in rural Georgia."

Stacey shook her head. "That's the worst of it. The best of it is all the love you get. There were so many people in my family, but nobody ever got lost in the shuffle. There was always somebody around to pay attention to us when we needed it."

"And now you're passing some of that on to my kids."

Stacey smiled at the tentative way Ryan had said the last two words. "It's a funny thing about love; the more you get, the more you keep trying to give it away."

"I can't believe there hasn't been a long line of young men with shopping bags held open for the pleasure, Georgia gal." He passed another quick glance over her slender body, lingering this time on her simple emerald halter top.

His words warming her blood, Stacey settled in to enjoy the familiar scenery, which eventually turned more and more mountainous. They passed stands advertising souvenirs and sourwood honey. A young boy boiling peanuts in a black iron kettle by the side of the road captured her attention, and she persuaded Ryan to stop and buy some for the children to snack on.

Deeply into the mountains of northern Georgia, they slowed their pace and ambled along the narrow mountain roads past fields of colorful day lilies and black-eyed susans. White wooden churches with peaked roofs and steeples posed against the green of the mountainsides, and craft stores advertising country handiwork were everywhere.

A rousing cheer shook the sleek blue sides of the van as they crossed the North Carolina border. To celebrate, they pulled over and ate their picnic lunch on a table hugging the edge of a mountaintop. Looking down, they could see fields of blue-green cabbages like straight-edged ponds with symmetrical waves.

When they got back into the van, Ryan consulted his map. "It will only be another hour and we'll be there," he informed them. "Everybody take a nap; you'll need lots of energy for setting up camp."

"Don't forget, we have to stop at the grocery store," Stacey reminded him as she shut her eyes.

Forty miles, five brown bags, and one consultation with a ranger later, they pulled up in front of a wooded site in a small camping area in the Nantahala National Forest. One hundred yards beyond, a wide creek bubbled cheerfully past. The setting was idyllic, with wild flowers growing in profusion in a meadow across the road from them and the jagged peaks of mountains visible from every angle.

"Everybody out," Ryan shouted, his face as enthusiastic as the children's. "Isn't this great?" he asked Stacey, his hand covering hers for a second.

"Quite a change from last night," she agreed, enjoying the warmth of this easy companionship. Whatever other strange vibrations there were between them, they were definitely becoming friends.

Ignoring the easiest places to pitch their tents, Ryan insisted that they carry their gear to the side of the creek and set up camp there. Although they would still cook and eat near the van, everything else had to be hauled the distance to their chosen tent sites. It took an hour, but with the children's cooperation they were finally comfortably established.

One moment of humor occurred when Ryan's childhood tent was removed from its shipping box. The tent weighed a ton; Ryan was right; they did not make them like they used to. Unfortunately, the tent was also full of tiny moth holes. When it was erected, the boys pushed their way in to investigate their new home only to discover that the sunlight was making dancing pinhole patterns on the rotting canvas floor. Ryan's mother thoughtfully had included a tent-patching kit in the package with the tent.

One tent-patching kit later only half the holes had been repaired. With an obnoxious, know-it-all grin, Stacey brought out the tent-patching kit that she had bought and put away for just such an emergency. "Do you think this will help?" she asked Ryan sweetly through the side of the tent. "I thought we might need it."

With a grunt that sounded like a bee-stung bear, Ryan held his hand out through a giant hole in one of the mosquito-netting windows. When he was finished, they spread an extra piece of canvas on the tent floor and zipped up the damaged window. As a peace offering, Stacey made a gallon of lemonade with clear, cold, mountain spring water, and they all sat to drink it at the picnic table.

"What I'd really like is a shower," Stacey said, yawning. The mountain air was definitely thinner and she could feel the changes in her own body as it adapted.

"I'm afraid I have bad news for you," Ryan admitted with a trace of sheepishness.

The campground did not have showers. In fact, the only running water was in the creek running by the back door of their tent. There was one hand-pumped water faucet for every six tent sites, and there were pit toilets.

"But I anticipated this." Ryan stood up and took a box out of the van. "It's a solar shower. You hang this in a tree and fill it up with water. Then the sun heats it, and when it's warm enough you turn it on and *voilà*, a shower."

This from the man who had refused to buy a camp stove to cook on. "If you think I'm going to take a shower in a clump of trees, Ryan Cunningham, you've lost your cotton-pickin' mind," Stacey snapped.

The children, however, had no such scruples. With a burst of speed they changed into bathing suits and as Ryan hauled water to the shower, they stood under the freezing-cold spring water screeching for more. Stacey contented herself with taking a sponge bath, fully clothed; Ryan contented himself with watching her take it.

The friendly teasing, the forced intimacy of performing everyday rituals together, and the laughter of the children seemed to bind Ryan and Stacey in a golden web of contentment. She tried to remember whether there had ever been a time in her life when she had felt so completely in harmony with a man. As they worked side by side, she seemed to know instinctively what Ryan needed from her. And when she needed something, Ryan was there immediately to provide it.

Harmony did not preclude excitement, however. Each time they touched each other as they performed a chore together, Stacey could feel each separate nerve ending pulse with joy. The small familiarities seemed to be building toward some profound conclusion that she couldn't even conceive of. Her body felt alive, as if it were reaching for some reality that she couldn't yet understand. But there was one thing she did know. The feelings she was developing for Ryan were not the feelings of a governess for her employer, or even of a woman for a man she respects. There was much, much more happening, at least from her viewpoint. And that knowledge was exhilarating.

Ryan started a small fire in the grill provided with the campsite. By the time it was ready, the sun had set behind the mountains, leaving their campsite encased in a rosy glow. They had grilled shish kebob of tender steak, fresh mushrooms, and tiny boiled potatoes, and they ate chunks of fresh tomatoes and cucumbers with it. To save washing dishes, Ryan suggested that they eat the entire meal with their fingers, and Stacey relished the sensual feel of the impromptu Tom Jones supper.

For dessert the children toasted marshmallows and ate them on graham crackers covered with thin slabs of chocolate, while Ryan and Stacey drank coffee made from water heated at length over the grill. The forest became a cacophony of crickets and frogs as the night closed in around them.

At the children's request, Ryan moved glowing coals to a stone circle close to their tents and built a roaring fire while Stacey and helpers cleaned up and put away their supplies. Washed clean and tucked into fleecy jogging suits for sleeping, the children sat on camp stools around the fire, warming their hands and frightening each other with stories about the sounds they heard.

Stacey changed into jeans and a heavy green sweater and emerged from the tent with a guitar case.

"Are you finally going to prove you can play that thing?" Ryan teased her. "I've been wondering why we were hauling it along."

Ignoring him, she unsnapped the latches and pulled out her guitar, gleaming golden brown in the firelight. Sitting on a stool, she tuned it carefully. "What songs do you know?" she asked the children.

They sang rousing choruses of "I've Been Working on the Railroad," "Dixie," and "This Old Man." Stacey's voice, a light, true soprano, led them easily, and she found with delight that Ryan, unlike most of the men she had known, enjoyed singing too.

"Let Stacey sing something by herself," Ryan requested, hands over his ears after the kids had sung twenty-five verses of "Found a Peanut."

She launched into the song that had won her the Miss Gainesville title: "Me and Bobby McGee." Like so many songs, it was about finding love and about the pain of losing it later. "Freedom's just another word for nothing left to lose," she sang, the familiar words biting into her consciousness as she voiced them. When she was finished, even the children were quiet for a moment, and only the soothing drone of insect voices was audible.

"You'd have made one terrific Miss America," Ryan said finally.

"And if I had won, I probably wouldn't be here right now," she answered softly. "Truthfully, there's no place else I'd rather be."

They finished up with "Old MacDonald Had a Farm." "When I was a kid," Stacey told the children, "we used to sing this every chance we got. My father's a farmer, and we had a sign in our yard that one of my brothers painted that said 'Old MacDonald's Farm.' When we got to the place in the song that says 'and on this farm he had some...' we'd shout 'kids' and then we'd go through the names of all the kids in the family, oldest to youngest."

"How many brothers and sisters do you have?" Caroline asked, her eyes round.

"Last time I heard," Stacey said with a chuckle, "there were twelve of us. Any my mother says that we were not cheaper by the dozen."

Jonathan wrinkled his freckled nose. "Yuck, eleven brothers and sisters!" He pretended to faint from the thought.

"Yep," Stacey agreed. "And there's even a set of twins, James and Randy. Imagine that."

"How old are the twins?" David asked with interest.

"Let's see." Stacey began to count on her fingers. "They're eight years younger than me, so that makes them fifteen."

"Can we meet them someday?" Jonathan asked.

Stacey flashed Ryan a plea for help. She could make no promises, because when the summer was over, the children would be gone from her life. She hated to remind them all of that fact.

"I think that's a good idea," Ryan intervened. "Maybe they'll set a good example and you can see how much better behaved you'll be in a few years." With a whoop the twins began to tickle him, and it was only after a fierce ten-minute battle that the children were persuaded to go to bed.

After getting the girls settled, Stacey carefully unzipped the tent and stepped outside, zipping it shut again. It was too early to follow the children to bed, and the campfire was still crackling, sending sparks up to meet the star-sprinkled blackness of the night. Ryan was nowhere to be seen, and Stacey, arms hugging her body for warmth in the chilling mountain air, squatted by the fire and stared into the flames.

"Cold, Stacey?" Ryan's voice came out of the blackness behind her, as if to warn her of his presence.

"A little," she admitted. "But the fire helps."

She saw him emerge from the shadows rolling a large log toward the fire. He positioned it carefully, close enough for warmth, distant enough for safety. "Come here," he said, motioning to her.

The log was big enough for two, but just barely. Ryan held out his arm as she perched tentatively on the edge, just brushing his body with hers. "Come closer," he said softly. "I'll warm you up."

There was no need to assure her of that fact. Being close to Ryan always warmed her up, whether she needed it or not. Stacey hesitated only momentarily. As if a life's decision was being made in a mere second's time, she nestled her soft curves next to his hard, lean body. The fit was perfect, and she leaned her head against his shoulder, accepting the warmth he was offering.

There was a soft intake of his breath, so soft that she thought she might have imagined it. His voice when it came was husky. "You feel so good. I guess I was cold too."

She had no idea how long they sat like that. Stacey was acutely aware of every sensation flooding her body: of the feel of his long, lean frame; of the tangible warmth wrapping itself around her; of the smell of wood smoke and the sound of crickets. Ryan's arm rested on her back and his hand curved along her rib cage, inches away from her breast; the internal reaction to his near-intimacy left her breathing in odd gulps.

It seemed like hours before Ryan finally broke the spell. "God, you're as soft as a kitten, cuddled up to me. Tell me, Georgia peach, why hasn't some man snatched you up like the sweet, delectable morsel that you are and carried you off to a vine-covered cottage?" He stood, bending over to draw another log into the dying fire.

The obvious answer to his question filled her in a rush, stunning her with its blinding clarity. It was quite simply because she had been biding her time, waiting all her life for Ryan Cunningham to appear. The silence lengthened as she gathered her defenses. There was no point in letting him know about her revelation; telling him her newly discovered feelings would accomplish nothing except to confuse them both. Wishing desperately for some time and space to examine her heart, Stacey hedged. The voice that finally answered him held only a hint of the inner turmoil she was experiencing, but her Georgia accent was thicker than usual. "I just never wanted to be carried off, I guess."

"It's funny," he said, his back still turned to her as he poked at the fire, sending new showers of sparks flying, "I believe strongly in equality for women, but I can't imagine you with a career. You were created to give pleasure to, and receive it from, a man and his children.''

"Sort of a dinosaur in the twentieth century,'' she murmured forlornly. "Born one hundred years too late.''

"That's not what I'm saying at all,'' he said, turning to face her. In the firelight the flickering shadows accented his high cheekbones and played with his smooth, tanned skin. "What I'm saying is that when I look at you I see roses growing on a trellis, and smell fresh peach pie baking in the oven, and hear the sounds of children playing happily in the background. Those aren't things to be ashamed of. I'm just wondering why you seem to be pursuing a different path.''

Perhaps the answer wasn't as simple as she had thought. No, she had never been in love before this—and that had made it easy to ignore the very things she treasured most—home, family, children. But she was close to being in love now, and even if Ryan grew to return her feeling, those things couldn't be hers. Her path had to be a different one. And the reason had to be her secret.

"If I never marry and have children of my own,'' she said carefully, "at least I will have been involved in children's lives. That's why I decided to become a teacher.''

"You'll be a good one, but you'd be a better mother. You give too much, way too much, and you're always going to have trouble letting go. You'll be a basket case every June.''

He wasn't the first person to tell her that. She remembered the quarter that she had done her student teaching in a little town in northern Florida. There had been one little boy in her class, all big eyes and shaggy hair, who had come to school every day in the same dirty, ragged shirt. Stacey had made a special effort to get close to him, to praise him when he did well and to cover up for him when he didn't. And every night she had gone back to the room in the old boarding house where she was staying and worried about him. Was he getting enough to eat? Were his parents abusing him?

Finally the teacher she was interning under had taken her aside for a heart-to-heart talk. The little boy was one of many just like him, she had told Stacey. He would disappear from her life in a few short weeks never to appear again, and there was nothing Stacey could do to change that. She could be kind, she could be gentle and considerate while he was in her sphere of influence; if she truly suspected abuse, she could report it. But poverty was not a crime, ragged clothes were not grounds for filing a report, not loving a child enough was not punishable by any authority. Stacey had to let go. She just had to let go.

She had, finally and with great difficulty, just as she would have to let go of Ryan's children at the end of the summer. But the constant letting go, the never being allowed to hold on, to cherish eternally, would take its final toll of her spirit. And it could never be any different.

She stood, arms crossed tightly in front of her again; the night had taken on a greater chill. "Nevertheless, I plan to teach. I'll just have to learn to handle the hard parts."

A protracted shiver wracked her, and Ryan was in front of her in a moment. "I'm sorry, Stacey. None of this was my business." His arms closed around her trembling body, pulling her to fit against him. The contact sent another chill coursing through her body. She tipped her head back to see his face, to apologize for the shivering, but the words died in her throat as they stood scant inches apart searching for some elusive truth in each other's eyes.

"With the moonlight on your hair," he murmured huskily, "you look like a wood nymph. Glowing skin, emerald eyes, shining hair." It was no surprise when his mouth sought hers. With her eyes open she saw his slow approach, felt his warm breath, tasted his sweetness almost before his lips touched hers. There was nothing playful about this kiss. It was a kiss of seduction, the kiss of a man for a woman he more than admires.

Ryan's tongue traced a searching path along the outline of her lips, moving gently in as she sighed and slowly opened her mouth for his pleasure. His arms wrapped tighter around her, bringing her to rest against him, his jean-clad thigh pressed between her legs. Stacey responded to the sensuous pressure by sighing again, straining closer to him until there was nothing between them except the softness of their sweaters.

When he ended the kiss, it was to begin another one, and this time she felt his hands under her sweater, lifting and kneading the flesh of her back through her T-shirt. She wished she wasn't wearing the shirt, a strange unbidden thought that would have shocked her back into awareness if Ryan's hands hadn't held quite the magic they did. Instead she found her own hands sliding under his sweater, contacting hard muscles and velvety skin. Ryan had come better prepared for this intimacy than she had.

He was all-pervading warmth, fluid marble to be explored and caressed, and she discovered each inch, stroking, circling, teasing lightly with her fingernails. The intimacy was brand new and exhilarating, and it fed pleasure through the sensitive receptors of her fingertips to every inch of her body.

"Stacey, do you know what you're doing, or have you been bewitched by the moonlight?" he murmured before he took her mouth again, this time with more pleasure, with more insistence.

It was a good question, but she didn't seem to be able to think of an answer. She stilled momentarily, her hands stopping their exploration, and with a ragged sign Ryan pulled away. "Sweet Georgia Brown," he breathed, "hasn't anyone ever told you that this stuff is habit-forming?"

She straightened, the movement taking her further from him. "You delight in making me feel as if I'm about twelve years old, don't you, Ryan? In case you haven't noticed, I'm a woman, fully grown."

"You may be a woman, but you're as innocent as a baby if you think that kind of behavior doesn't lead to something." He was grinning at her now, his strong, straight teeth framed by the up-curved lips that had just given her such pleasure.

She couldn't share in the teasing, even though she imagined it was Ryan's way of cooling off the dangerous passion that had flared so briefly between them. Her hazel eyes luminous, she stepped back.

"Well, I'll spare you any further attacks of wanton behavior. Good night." She turned to find her way back to the tent. In a split second he had her by the arm, spinning her around to face him again.

"Don't ever assume," he said almost coldly, "that your wanton behavior displeases me. But we have a month of nights like this ahead of us, and I've sworn to your cousin that you will be the same, sweet Stacey MacDonald when I return you to her doorstep. Tread carefully, Georgia peach. I hate to break my word." As if to erase his gruffness, he moved to stand closer to her. "Now, say good-night." He brushed a kiss on her lips, lingering just a fraction of a second too long for it to be casual.

"Good night, Ryan," she said, her voice sounding far away.

"Pleasant dreams," he whispered as he let her go. "God knows, I hope mine will be pleasant too."

Chapter Five

Dew covered the grass outside their tents in pristine, jewellike droplets, and fine, smoky mist covered the landscape, giving the campsite an ethereal beauty that was too lovely to ignore. Careful not to wake anyone else, Stacey unzipped the tent flap and eased herself outside. It was very early—the sun had not even made it over the high peaks of the mountains—but the scenery through the haze was suffused with a glow that promised eventual sunshine.

After a stop at what passed for the bathroom, she followed a foot-worn path beside the creek, pretending that she was a Cherokee Indian brave hunting game. Her masquerade was rewarded when upstream, far away from the campground, she saw two does on the other side of the creek. Noiselessly she sat on a rock watching them drink the icy mountain water. One of the deer raised its graceful head and looked directly at Stacey. Its tail flicked in answer to the reassuring look in her eyes. Finally, without excitement, the two deer wandered back into the forest.

The creek was wide and the water knee-deep. Stacey could see wide, smooth stones on the bottom, and without a second thought, she took off her sneakers and rolled her pant legs up to her thighs. But there were two things she had not taken into consideration. The stones were slippery and the water was flowing at a rate only perfect balance could contend with. "Oh, well, I needed a bath anyway," she muttered from her new position, bottom down on the creek floor.

The water flowed over her shoulders and up to her chin, and she was quickly numbed by the freezing temperature. "Might as well go all the way," she pronounced cheerfully as she ducked her head, wet honey hair floating around her.

"Stacey, stay there, I'm coming." The words came to her as through a thick blanket, and she lifted her head quickly to find their source. Ryan was charging over the slippery creek bottom like Don Quixote toward his windmills. The only difference was that Ryan was swearing, a reaction that she would not have expected from a windmill charger.

"For Pete's sake, Ryan, I'm fine," she yelled, standing up carefully. "Be careful, you're going to fall!" Helplessly she watched her prophecy come true.

He surfaced slowly. Guess the number of goose bumps on this irresistible male's body and win the grand prize, she thought with the beginning of a hysterical giggle. Fist covering her mouth, she turned away, trying desperately to control her laughter. Strong hands came to rest on her shoulders, and Ryan was turning her gently. "It's all right, Stacey. You'll be fine when you dry off."

"Oh, Ryan," she exploded in helpless waves of mirth. "You looked so funny."

The icy water had slowed his reaction time. He stared at her in disbelief while his frozen brain added up the evidence. Stacey was not hurt. She was not upset. She was laughing at him. "Georgia gal, you've had it now," he said menacingly. With a shove she was back in the water, but not before she had grasped his intention and hooked her hands under his arms. The slippery rocks won again and Ryan was in the water too.

She wrestled herself out from under his body, scrambling for the shore, but he grabbed the tail of her sweater and pulled her back to land on his lap. Reaching behind him, she locked her arms around his back, pushing the creek bottom with her feet to duck them both. Under the water he turned her over, hauling her up like a frozen sack of potatoes to throw her over his shoulder. After several outrageous threats he finally carried her to the shore.

They were both shivering when he set her down, and she clung shakily to him for warmth. "Just tell me one thing," he ground out between tremors. "What in hell were you doing in that water?"

"Fishing?" she asked tentatively. "Would you believe I was doing it Indian style, without a fishing pole?" His arms tightened around her, and even with their combined shivering she could feel a strong reaction to his nearness forming in the pit of her stomach.

"Let's get you back to the campsite," he said finally, his hands absentmindedly exploring her curves through the wet, clinging sweater. "You'll catch pneumonia if you don't warm up."

"I think I'm warming up already," she said, tilting her chin to read his expression. His own reaction was plain to see. With a jolt she realized that she affected Ryan Cunningham too. And with another jolt, she realized that he was fighting that attraction with every fiber of his being.

"Sweet Stacey, let's go." He grunted, releasing her quickly to head down the path in the direction of their tents.

The girls were just waking up when she unzipped the tent flap. She dried herself quickly, rubbing her arms and legs to increase their sluggish circulation. The day was warming up, but she dressed in jeans and a college sweatshirt to be sure that her chill would disappear rapidly enough.

Ryan had already started a fire in the grill when she and the girls came out of their tent. David and Jonathan were up and exploring the meadow across the road with a new friend from a nearby campsite. "I though you didn't like breakfast," she commented as she got out bacon and eggs to cook over the fire.

"For some reason, my appetite was awakened earlier than usual. Must have been that bracing morning swim."

"I'm sorry, Ryan," she said, trying not to smile. "But no one has ever rescued me before. I'll treasure that memory of you racing through the water to save me." Her voice broke into helpless giggles.

Luckily, Ryan was awake enough to see the humor in the situation, and he smiled benignly at her. "Do you have any idea how silly you looked sitting in the middle of that creek with your head under the water?"

"Do you know that when you thought I was drowning, you yelled at me to stay there?" she said, her giggles turning into sobs of laughter. "Where on earth did you think I was going to go?" She shut her eyes, making a heroic effort to control herself. When she opened them Ryan was towering over her.

"Not another word, Stacey," and as if to make sure that she obeyed him, he covered her mouth with his. The kiss, surprise that it was, was the highlight of her morning.

Their predawn experience in the creek was not to be their last. After a morning spent playing with a Frisbee and exploring mountain paths, Ryan bundled their bathing-suit-clad bodies into the van for a mysterious trip up the road. At a weatherbeaten shack by the side of the creek they rented inner tubes and, after careful instruction and securing life jackets, they waded into the water, climbed into their inner tubes, and set off downstream.

Christy, in a special tube with a solid bottom, was securely anchored between Stacey and Ryan. The little girl sat placidly watching the scenery drift by as if tubing was an everyday occurrence.

The hot summer sun beat down on them, and the icy water rose to meet only parts of their bodies. It was a lazy, sensuous afternoon, the tubes rocking gently, the water nipping at their bottoms and their feet. The panorama of the mountains around them made it a perfect experience.

"I've never done this before," Stacey said, breaking the comfortable silence. "I feel as if I'm in heaven."

"Have you ever been to the mountains before?" Ryan asked, turning on his side to watch her.

She briefly admired his tan, lean body, emphasized by the short cut-offs, his bare chest covered with fine, curly hair tapering to a V as it grazed the band of his shorts. A flicker of excitement, not abated by the cold water or the lazy atmosphere, ran through her. "No," she said with a sigh. "Farmers just don't take vacations. Especially when they have twelve kids. Have I been so dreadfully obvious?"

"You've been like a kid at the circus. It's been lovely to watch."

She blushed at the compliment. "This probably sounds crazy, but I've always known that when I finally got to the mountains, I'd feel right at home. Maybe it's because they're so near to where I grew up, but I've always known that when I finally got to see them up close they would seem as if they belonged to me."

"I'm glad to be the one who brought you here, then. I like giving you pleasure." Their eyes caught and held, until finally he turned away to maneuver their tubes to avoid a fallen tree trunk lying sideways in the water.

His last words curled up deep inside her to radiate warmth throughout her body for the rest of the afternoon.

As it turned out, warmth was what they all needed. After dragging their tubes out of the icy creek, they dried off and changed into warm clothes just in time to be drenched again by a chilling mountain rainstorm. Ryan jogged up the road in the rain to retrieve the van while Stacey and the children scurried around moving their supplies to shelter. With a groan she ripped open a plastic trash bag and anchored it on top of their pile of firewood, but it was too late; the wood was soaked.

Again they changed clothes, huddling together in Stacey's tent while the rain poured down in torrents. After muddy footprints were wiped up and sleeping bags were rolled out to accommodate them, they played Old Maid while Christy, exhausted by the day's events, slept soundly in the corner. On a small Sterno stove that Stacey had hidden away, they heated water and made hot chocolate. The sound of the rain was reassuring, lessening as the afternoon slipped by.

Ryan arrived after what seemed like hours, soaked and bone-weary. Mountain jogging, it seemed, was not like jogging in the gentle hills of Tallahassee. He gratefully accepted a cup of hot chocolate and changed into dry clothes while everyone kept their eyes squeezed shut. Stacey breathed deeply and practiced stern self-control during the whole tantalizing episode.

Finally the rain slowed to a mere drizzle. "I think we'd better start some dinner," Stacey said, twisting a lock of hair, one of many that had been made unruly by the rain.

The firewood was entirely too wet to use; the one can of Sterno that had come with the stove was gone. Dinner consisted of peanut butter and jelly sandwiches and potato chips. And the fact that they were able to fix it at all was a small miracle, because immediately afterward the rain began again. Once more they took shelter in Stacey's tent, abandoning Old Maid to concentrate on Twenty Questions.

Luckily, the day's excitement had tired them all, and when the darkness of the storm combined with the darkness of evening, the children went to bed willingly. Stacey lay awake for a long time listening to the rain bombard the canvas roof. Ryan's words of the night before came back to haunt her. "We have another month of nights like this," he had said as the velvety darkness had surrounded them. If it continued to rain, Stacey was sure that they would never have to test their self-control again. And if that was probably for the best, why did she feel so disappointed?

The next week was spent under raincoats trying to stay dry. Eventually those were shed, not because it had stopped raining but because everyone was still getting wet anyway. Saturated and miserable, they sloshed through their campsite, trying to ignore the insistent drops that pelted their bodies. By the second day, everyone hated Old Maid; by the third day, peanut butter sandwiches were out of favor; by the fourth day, the children were fighting over toys, books, and anything else they could find to fight over.

Ryan's tent began to leak during the first night. The holes were not so large as to need much patching, but the canvas was too wet to repair. They contented themselves with taking turns mopping up the small puddles as they collected around the door of the tent. On the second night, they were mopping faster. By the fourth night, they were mopping every half hour.

On the morning of the fifth day, Stacey sat at the picnic table, hardly noticing the fine drizzle in the air. "This is going to be the day that it clears up," she told Ryan as he emerged from mopping his tent.

The look he gave her would have killed a rattlesnake at twenty paces. "How you can sit there looking serene and cheerful with the rain coming down all around you is beyond me!''

She ignored his bad humor, running her fingers through her hair, which by this time was curling in wet tendrils all the way down to her shoulders. "At least it's not cold. I'd really be worried if it were. A little water won't hurt anybody," she reasoned calmly.

"I'm not trying to be nasty," he said nastily, "but have you been reading *Pollyanna* to the children?"

She ignored him again. "I think we should take a hike this afternoon. Even it it's still raining, at least it will get us away from the tents for a while."

"I think *you* should take a hike," he said shortly, disappearing into his tent, which by this time was indistinguishable from a swimming pool.

The boys moved into the girls' tent that night. Supposedly the tent was able to accommodate four adults. With four children and one adult it was wall-to-wall sleeping bags. Ryan slept in the van alone.

Throwing up his hands in disgust, Ryan took them all out for breakfast the next morning. They drove forever before they found an open cafe in a sleepy little town miles from their campsite. Bedraggled at best, they were almost turned away at the door, but the proprietor's wife took pity on them and sat them in the back of the empty room.

With her hands wrapped around the first cup of hot liquid that she had consumed in days, Stacey stared across the table at Ryan. "Well?" she asked. "What next?"

"The weather forecast insists that this front has almost passed through. Can you make it another day or two?" His curls were springing around his face, outlining in sharp relief the prominent bone structure and the heavy-lidded eyes. Stacey fought down an urge to reach up and twine his hair around her finger.

"Sure, I'm doing fine," she answered. "The kids will be fine just as soon as the rain stops. They're tired of being cooped up."

"So am I. We're spending all our time just trying to survive and keep as dry as possible. It hasn't exactly been a vacation." He leaned back in his chair, jean-clad knees brushing Stacey's as he did.

It was the first physical contact they had made since the day the rain had started. Stacey had spent her spare time since that day convincing herself that she was imagining all the electricity between them. A simple brush of his knees destroyed her theory. Electricity could be explained. She supposed that there were many men in the world who could generate this physical excitement within her. The trouble was that she had never met any of those other men. And if she ever did, there was a good chance she wouldn't even like them. She knew she liked Ryan Cunningham.

In fact, she more than liked him. That night under the stars she had imagined she was falling in love. Today, rain soaked and miserable, she was sitting across a linoleum table from him in a two-bit cafe, eating greasy eggs and dried-out bacon, and she knew she was in love. Why else was this the only place in the world that she wanted to be?

"Stacey?" Ryan asked quietly, his eyes watching the expressions flicker across her face. "What are you thinking about?"

"About stars and dried-out bacon," she said a little breathlessly. About love and how impossible it is, she added silently.

"Mommy," Christy screeched from the high chair at the end of the table.

Ryan watched Stacey slide half the contents of her plate onto Christy's now empty one. "She's still calling you Mommy," he commented as she came back to her seat.

"I know." Stacey sighed. "I'm trying to get her to call me Stacey, but sometimes she forgets. Does it bother you?"

"I think," he said softly, "that it suits you."

His words settled over Stacey's spirit like the dark clouds drifting outside the dingy cafe windows. Perhaps being a mother suited her, but it would never be possible.

They held on for two more days. Occasionally the sun came out, sometimes long enough to begin drying some of the deep puddles that had formed throughout the campground. Always, though, it declined to stay, resorting to hiding behind dark clouds that once again showered them with sheets of driving rain.

"I know how Noah felt," Ryan growled after an entire wet week had passed.

"I know how you feel about giving the children a real camping experience," Stacey said soothingly, "and I think your idea was a very good one."

"But?"

"But it's not working." She passed her hand through her hair, which was beginning to dry in fluffy tangles all over her head. One glance at the sky assured her that she would not need to comb it; in an hour's time it would be wet again.

"If the rain hasn't stopped tomorrow, we'll do something about it," Ryan promised her. "Have I told you that you're a terrific sport?"

The compliment pleased her. If it was not exactly what she would like to hear from him, it was still nice.

They finished up the jar of peanut butter and the last can of tuna fish huddled in Stacey's tent that evening listening to the rain. Ryan had gone for a walk, or a slosh, as Caroline renamed it, while the children practiced feeling sorry for themselves.

"My sleeping bag's wet again," David complained.

"Mine's never been dry," Jonathan whined.

Stacey traded with Jonathan, although her bag was wet too. Caroline unzipped hers and David shared it with her. Stacey covered them with a blanket that was only slightly damp. Unzipping Jonathan's bag, Stacey turned it inside out and covered it with her raincoat, preparing to sleep without rolling over.

It was a while before everyone was quiet, but finally the eternally dripping rain was the only noise audible...except for the creek. The musical sound of the creek usually lulled Stacey to sleep, but that night it sounded decidedly unmusical. Carefully picking her way across sleeping children, she pulled on her raincoat and stepped out into the rain, shivering at the chill. She had forgotten her flashlight, and rather than risk waking the children she stood outside under a makeshift canvas shelter until her eyes could pick out the now familiar landmarks. Silently she made her way down to the water's edge.

There was a shape she didn't recognize by the side of the creek. When it moved suddenly, she jumped backward, ready to race back to the campsite. "Stacey, come here."

"Ryan, you scared me to death. What are you doing?" she asked in relief.

"The same thing you are, I imagine." He motioned for her to come and stand beside him. "The creek's rising. I've been watching it all day, and I don't like the looks of it."

"If there was a real problem, wouldn't they tell us?" she questioned him.

"I've talked to the ranger. They're monitoring it carefully, and we aren't in any real danger...yet."

"Should we leave?" she asked faintly.

"We should have left days ago." Her eyes had adjusted well enough to see his features in between the constant drops of rain. Ryan was not happy with himself. "I wanted this camping trip to be really special for the kids, and I just didn't know when to quit."

"They've gotten something out of it," she said, trying to be helpful.

"What?" He snorted.

"Wet!" she blurted before she could stop herself.

Ryan's husky laughter bubbled from his toes up, surprising them both. Two sodden bodies came together, rain-soaked eyelashes hiding the very real feeling beneath their friendly embrace. "Georgia gal," she heard him say as she stood with her head pressed to his chest, "you are definitely one of a kind."

They walked back to the campsite arms entwined. "I'm not going to sleep in the van tonight," Ryan announced at the door of the tent. "I want to stay close to the creek so that I can monitor what's going on."

"Your tent is soaked," Stacey said worriedly. "You'll be sleeping in a huge puddle if you stay there."

"I know. I'm going to sleep in your tent."

"There's no room, Ryan," she said, her body reacting to the thought of him sleeping near her by flushing with heat.

"We'll have to make room," he answered calmly. "Unzip the tent, Stacey."

There was only one place available and it was between Stacey and Jonathan. In addition to everything else, it gave Ryan the best shot at the tent flap so that he could avoid disturbing anyone when he went to check on the creek.

"Can you spread out that sleeping bag?" Ryan asked her after rolling the sleeping children closer together.

She nodded, moving through the ritual as if in a trance. The sleeping bag was unzipped and fluffed as best it could be while Ryan squatted down on his heels watching her. She tried to joke. "You'll be sorry; I'm told I kick and squirm all night."

"And tell me, who would know those details?"

She blushed, glad that it was too dark for him to see. "My sisters, of course."

"Of course."

As calmly as she could, Stacey removed her raincoat and her sneakers. Next to go was her sweater, leaving her in a T-shirt and soft wet jogging pants. There was nothing else to do. She lay down, pulling the blanket over her tremulous body, and watched Ryan undress.

His raincoat hit the ground, followed by shoes and sweater. Unlike Stacey, however, he didn't stop, removing a clinging, wet T-shirt and rain-soaked pants. As he stood stripped down to nothing but briefs, his sheer masculinity overpowered her. She shut her eyes.

"Stacey," he whispered, as he lay down beside her. "I understand your innate modesty, but if you don't get those wet pants off, I'm going to take them off for you."

He was right, the jogging pants were soaked, but the thought of lying there practically unclothed next to him was just too much. "I'm fine," she insisted. "They'll dry right away."

"Off, or I'll take them off."

She inched the pants down, hiding under the miserable little blanket. "There," she almost spat, "are you satisfied?"

"That's a funny question," he answered turning toward her. "Now come here and share that blanket."

"Find your own blanket," she said, wide-eyed in the darkness.

"Share, Stacey."

She felt his body closing in on her, his hands reaching for the scratchy wool of the blanket. "All right," she squeaked, "here, take it."

Her body was encircled by his, and frantically she turned on her side away from him. He tucked the blanket around them both, moving closer to her as he did so. To her feverish mind, he seemed to be touching every part of her, spreading his body heat everywhere his body melted into hers.

With a low sound of pleasure he draped his arm over her chest. If his fingers dangled even an inch closer, it would have been perfectly acceptable to slap them away. As it was, she lay rigid in his arms, wishing that she could breathe normally again.

"There, isn't that better?" he murmured, his face hidden in her silky hair.

"Better than what?" she squeaked again.

"Calm down, Stacey, I'm not going to do anything. Just let me hold you tonight. Just this once let me hold you."

She was sure that he could feel her heart racing and the very real tension in every muscle of her body. It could be no more romantic than sleeping with an alarm clock, she decided, but Ryan didn't seem to mind. He snuggled even closer.

"So sweet," he said as he drifted off to sleep. "My sweet little Georgia peach."

Chapter Six

There were long, tapering fingers draped over her breasts, just tantalizing a taut nipple, when she awoke the next morning. Stacey could feel the hardness of Ryan's body curled around hers, and she realized with horrified surprise that she had cuddled up to him in the night so tightly that there was no space between them at all.

"Whoever told you that you kick and squirm was pulling your leg," a sensuous voice whispered in her ear. "You snuggle and sigh like a little girl with her favorite teddy bear. Sleeping with you is a fabulous experience."

Stacey didn't feel like a little girl. With his fingers brushing her breast and his warmth melting into her, she felt like a woman on the edge of losing her virtue. And the worst part was that she was trying desperately to remember why that was so bad.

"Turn over and give me a good-morning kiss, Georgia gal." He rolled her toward him with an easy motion. His muscular bare leg settled over her, pulling her close.

For a moment they were lying face to face in the most intimate of positions. Stacey could barely breathe.

Her breasts, unrestrained under the T-shirt, were pressing against his bare chest, and her legs, caught between his, were long lengths of highly sensitized skin. She could feel every muscle of his body tensed against her unresisting flesh. And even though her experience with men was limited, she knew that Ryan was as aroused by her as she was by him.

By degrees, she relaxed against him, allowing her body to move against his. She heard him catch his breath, and when she lifted her head she saw that his heavy-lidded eyes were glazed with desire.

"Did you know that early in the morning your eyes are the color of jade?" Ryan asked, his voice no longer teasing. "Sometimes they're topaz, and sometimes they're jade." He seemed to witness her internal struggle. "And sometimes they're very, very frightened." His kiss was gentle, taking the sweetness that she offered, savoring it, and returning it again. She could feel his heart pounding, and she knew that hers was pounding just as fast.

"Uncle Ryan, it's very wet over here," said a small voice from the other side of the tent. "I don't want to camp anymore." As if they had all been waiting for this opportunity to express themselves, the other waking children began to chime in. "I want to go back to Florida. This is no fun." Even Christy added, "No fun."

Ryan had turned from Stacey at the sound of the first little voice and was pulling on his pants under the blanket. "You're all right. But we can't go back to Florida yet. Right now our house doesn't have a roof." His response was met by a chorus of groans.

Stacey turned, unobtrusively dressing as the children hurled complaints at their uncle. She tied her damp sneakers with fingers that were not quite steady, and she silently said a prayer of gratitude that there were four tiny chaperones in the tent.

"Kids, we aren't staying here another night, I promise. Not with that creek rising," Ryan said to mollify them.

"Where are we going?" Stacey asked, her curiosity piqued.

"A friend of mine is a realtor in Highlands; she's going to rent us a cabin in a valley near there. We'll be dry and comfortable if it keeps raining and in a beautiful part of the mountains for exploring if it doesn't."

They packed up in the rain, hardly noticing the big drops they were so excited at leaving. Although they had gone into town several times to do laundry, it was to wash and dry their sleeping bags, and so Stacey had nothing left to wear that wasn't wet or muddy.

I was almost Miss Georgia? she asked herself as she caught sight of her reflection in the big side-view mirror of the van. Her hair was wet, hanging in limp strands down past her shoulders. Her face was pale and streaked with mud and she was dressed in blue jeans that could only be described as filthy.

Ryan was wet too. His clothes were not clean, and there was a spot of mud on his forehead. But even rumpled and wet, Ryan looked terrific. Stacey was sure she would never look terrific again.

Anxious to get to Highlands, they stopped and bought sausage, biscuits and orange juice, and breakfasted in the van. Caroline sat beside Ryan, and Stacey sat in the back with the children to help Christy with the impromptu meal. The mountains became more rugged, the road more winding, and the scenery more exquisite. They passed waterfalls spilling entire rivers over rock precipices. The forests were full of rhododendron in bloom, pale pink blossoms like spun cotton candy against waxy green leaves. Nothing in the mountains was ordinary; even simple things stood out in the symphony of color and form.

The tiny town of Highlands was a delight. It was a town that cared about itself. Admittedly it was a town that had to care because its primary business was tourism, but Highlands, unlike some of the settlements in the nearby Great Smoky Mountains, was a tasteful melding of understated elegance and natural beauty. Red geraniums hanging in pots and petunias planted around white clapboard buildings graced the narrow main street. Expensive shops crowded the sidewalk, and summer residents strolled past, admiring displays as they stopped to gossip with each other.

Ryan pulled the van into a diagonal parking space across the street from a pink brick building with a sign that assured them that all their real estate needs would soon be met. "Come on in, everybody," Ryan said. "This may take a while."

Stacey took one look at her dirty jeans and shook her head, but Ryan insisted. "I want you to meet MyraLou," he said. "I'm sure you'll like her. She's very friendly."

MyraLou was indeed a friendly person...friendly to men. Stacey's heart sank as she took her first look at this paragon. MyraLou was perfect in a Junior League and afternoon-tea-on-Wednesday sort of way. Her hair was blond—not a mixture of blond and brown and who knows what else like Stacey's hair, but blond, each strand the same identical shade of off-white. It was pulled back in a perfect chignon to expose a face with makeup faultlessly applied to emphasize wide blue eyes. Her clothes had just come out of a Highland's shop window: a perfect red cotton pullover blouse and a white wraparound skirt with a red-apple appliqué to match.

"Why, Ryan," she said when Stacey had been introduced. "Wherever did you pick up this charming child? What a good idea it was to hire a high-school student to be your baby-sitter this summer." MyraLou looked up at Ryan and batted her long eyelashes. "But I'm surprised her mother would let you near such a sweet young thing, with your naughty reputation." She turned back to examine Stacey, who took in the slight narrowing of the lovely blue eyes. Stacey choked down her rising animosity. She would not play that game.

Ryan's arm was around the friendly person, and he squeezed the red pullover as he scolded her. "Stacey isn't a child; she's a good friend who, out of the goodness of her heart, is helping this bachelor with his four children for the summer."

"Why, how kind of you, dear," MyraLou gushed, her eyes narrowing to slits. "You must be the maternal type."

How being the maternal type could sound like an Egyptian mummy's curse was beyond Stacey's comprehension, but it did when it came out of MyraLou's geranium-red lips. "Just call me Ma Kettle," Stacey said sweetly. "Ryan, if you don't mind, I think we'll wait for you outside. David and Jonathan want to look around a little."

Ryan followed them outside later, too much later for comfort, Stacey thought as she saw him bend and kiss MyraLou in the open doorway. MyraLou's eyes were gleaming as she waved, sold gold bangles jingling. "Good-bye, Stacey. Lovely to have met you. I'm sure you'll adore the cabin. It has plenty of soap and hot water and a washer and dryer too."

They were five miles out of town before Stacey cooled off. Washer and dryer indeed. She entertained herself with thoughts of what MyraLou would look like after a week of camping in the rain with four children. That artificially blond hair would not look so chic if it were mud-encrusted. Without her resort wear, MyraLou would probably look...great. MyraLou, wet and dirty, would still be gorgeous. Stacey realized with a sad thump that she had been completely outclassed. So much for revengeful thoughts.

Six miles out of town, Stacey temporarily forgot about Ryan kissing MyraLou and watched in wonder as more magnificent scenery unfolded. They were now on a gravel road lined with towering hardwood trees and occasional cabins. Sometimes they got a glimpse of a sheer granite cliff and Ryan told her that it was Whiteside Mountain, one of the oldest mountains in North America.

Gunning the motor, Ryan pulled the van up a steep gravel driveway that eventually leveled out and dipped back down. At the little road's end was a log cabin nestled comfortably in a clump of maple and poplar trees. "Everybody out," he announced as he pulled the van into a turnaround at the end of the drive.

"Ryan, are you serious?" Stacey asked.

He turned and studied her face. "Is this the same young woman who camped for a week in the rain without complaining once? Is a log cabin such a comedown?"

She was surprised that he had misunderstood. "Oh, no! It's wonderful." Her eyes were lit up like the sky on a clear mountain night. "I just never thought I'd have the chance to stay someplace like this. It's perfect."

The side of his index finger brushed her cheek, probably smearing whatever mud she hadn't managed to get off. "I'm glad I can share it with you, then, Georgia gal."

Inside, the cabin was perfect too. Entering through the big front porch they stepped into the living room whose wide-planked oak floors had been polished to a high shine by years of soft footsteps. The living room had a fieldstone fireplace that was large enough to heat the entire cabin, and perched on one side of the high-ceilinged room was a loft with a solid railing tall enough to keep children from falling over.

There was an instant fight over who would get to sleep in the loft. Ryan finally decided that they would have to rotate, the twins claiming the first night. The rest of the cabin was roomy and solid, with two bedrooms and a huge bathroom that to Stacey, who had forgotten what having indoor plumbing was like, looked as if it had come straight out of a women's magazine. In the back, behind a well-planned kitchen with all the modern conveniences, was a large room with another fireplace and picture windows that brought the breathtaking view of Whiteside Mountain inside. A low deck with wraparound seating completed the plan.

"Did you design this, Ryan?" Stacey asked.

He shook his head. "No, this cabin is much older than I am. But I was up here once visiting MyraLou, and I was consulted a little on the renovations. The cabin's been in her family for years, but she never uses it. It's for sale."

Stacey couldn't imagine anyone in his or her right mind selling the place. If it had been hers, she would have moved heaven and earth to keep it. But she could see that it would have no appeal for MyraLou. "I hope whoever buys it loves it," she said with deep feeling.

They carried their belongings indoors, piling everything that was wet or dirty on the front porch, which meant that very little actually came inside. Since the sun was shining and the dark clouds of the last week seemed to have drifted into oblivion, Stacey and Ryan spread the tents out to dry in the front yard. With a minimum of fuss, they sorted and washed and settled in. After a long, hot shower and donning clean jeans and a pink tank top, Stacey felt like a new woman.

As if the rain understood that they were now safe from its ravages, the next week was cloud-free. To make up to all of them for the abortive camping trip, Ryan made it his personal project to be sure that they had a good time. They explored mountain trails, stopping at the foot of waterfalls to play in the sparkling pools. Ryan and the older children fished in mountain streams for fresh trout and brought their catch home to Stacey, who could clean and cook a fish quicker than a fast-food restaurant could grill a hamburger.

They visited Highlands and nearby Cashiers and poked around the gem stores and the expensive boutiques and craft shops. One day they drove to the nearby Cowee

Valley and visited a mine to try their hand at prospecting for sapphires and rubies. Sitting out in an open field with the blazing sun burning through her plaid blouse, Stacey looked around and knew that she had never been happier.

The children and Ryan were clustered around the raised wooden trough that pushed water rapidly past them so that they could wash the dirt that they had bought by the bucketful. Caroline was taking the escapade seriously, certain, beyond the shadow of a doubt, that she would find a perfectly faceted twenty-carat ruby glittering up at her from her screened pan.

It was Stacey, however, who found a ruby. It was a tiny one, so tiny, in fact, that it had lodged under her fingernail when she swished her pan out in disgust for the last time. But it shone a clear, cherry red, and to all of them it was the most beautiful thing they had ever seen. The old woman who worked at the mine laughed at their excitement as she stooped to dig casually through the piles of tiny rocks at Caroline's feet. A second later she presented the awestruck little girl with a genuine sapphire chip, not like anything any of them had ever seen, but a guaranteed sapphire nonetheless.

"These are hard to spot," she told Caroline, "but this one is definitely yours. It was practically on your toe."

They stopped at one of the many jewelers lining the streets of Franklin, the town nearby noted as a gem center, and bought a gold chain with a glass bubble in which to put the ruby and sapphire. Caroline wore it with the pride that only a child is capable of. Ryan teased Stacey all the way back to the cabin because she insisted on hauling back the dirt that they had bought and not had time to screen.

"You'll wish you hadn't laughed when Caroline and I find a ruby worth millions in this dirt," she said smugly.

"It's costing me millions just to haul it back," he teased.

Ryan's mood for the whole week had been excellent. With the children he was warm and funny, playing his role as the doting uncle-turned-father to the hilt. The palpable tensions that had permeated the air in Florida had disappeared, leaving them room to begin to forge the bonds of a new family. The bonds were still tentative, but every day they seemed to strengthen and grow.

The bonds between Stacey and the children were strengthening too, even though she knew that she should begin to pull back a little. Perhaps she could have distanced herself if she hadn't been so afraid of hurting them, but they had lost so much that she couldn't bear to cause them more pain. When the children approached her for comfort or for love she tried to turn them toward Ryan, but if he wasn't available, she provided them with what she could. And every day she grew to care about them more.

Without the forced intimacy of the camping experience, Ryan and Stacey were able to maintain their own distance. There was no repetition of the passionate embraces or exploratory kisses of their camping week. They played together, did chores together, and took care of the children's needs together. But beyond those limited contacts, Ryan seemed to be avoiding her. At times Stacey wondered if she had just imagined the morning in the tent with Ryan's arms encircling her.

Nowadays, Ryan's arms were busy encircling MyraLou. Or at least that was what Stacey surmised went on in the evenings after the children were in bed and Ryan left for Highlands. Since they'd taken up residence there, he had not remained in the cabin once after the sun set over Whiteside Mountain; he would leave MyraLou's number in case of emergency and trot off to be with her.

Stacey, who had thought herself above petty jealousy, was stricken with as bad a case as was possible to catch. It was true that Ryan came home each night to sleep, but even the limited hours he was spending with MyraLou were driving Stacey to distraction.

It was the harsh reality of her reaction to his nightly rendezvous that finally convinced her she was in love. Only love could make her feel this bad. Only love could make her lose her sense of humor.

"What are you looking so glum about, Georgia peach?" Ryan teased one morning as they lingered over coffee, listening to the shouts of the children who were outside kicking a soccer ball back and forth.

"I'm just daydreaming," she said with a blink. Ryan, dressed in an olive-drab safari shirt that was unbuttoned halfway down his chest, was not looking glum. He was looking sexy and very content. "You look like the cat who swallowed the canary," she said accusingly. "You must be having a very enjoyable week."

"Now why would the Georgia gal say that as if an enjoyable week was a bad thing to have?" he mused out loud, watching Stacey with a slow grin. "Have I been doing something I should be ashamed of?"

"How should I know?" she snapped, getting up from the table to finish clearing off their breakfast dishes. "It's not my business if you want to have an enjoyable week. Go ahead. See if it bothers me!" Bite your tongue, a cautious internal voice warned her.

"Stacey," his voice sounded from directly behind her, low and sensuous. "Tell Uncle Ryan what's bothering you." His arms encircled her waist, pulling her back to lean against him.

"You are not my uncle, Ryan," she said coldly, trying not to let his casual embrace muddle her thinking.

"That's true, I'm not," he agreed, his mouth nuzzling her ear. "Aren't you glad?"

"It makes no difference to me," she said shortly. "No difference at all."

"Then why is your heart beating so fast, Georgia peach? It's speeding like a rock band drummer with a two-minute solo."

"Give me a break, Ryan," she said, giving up the pretense of anger. "I'm not like most of the women you know; I don't take this kind of contact lightly. Please remove your hands."

She felt him step back, leaving a wide void between them, and she turned around slowly to face him. She owed him some sort of an explanation for her behavior, even if it wasn't a complete one. "I'm sorry I'm in a bad mood. Maybe having all this fun just doesn't agree with me."

"And maybe something else is bothering you," he murmured, rubbing his finger lightly down the side of her face. "What's really wrong?"

She shook her head, acutely aware of how much she wanted to throw herself into his arms and ask to be held fully against him. Standing there with his dark hair curling around his face and his powerful body leaning toward her, Ryan was magnificent, a man worth making a food of herself for. But Stacey MacDonald didn't have the courage to do anything except lie. "Everybody deserves an occasional grouchy day. I guess this is mine," she whispered. "I'm sorry."

"Chin up, Georgia gal. I'll take care of it for you," he said. She expected a kiss, it was tangible in the air between them, but Ryan had evidently taken her protest at his embrace seriously. He declined to touch her. "Go put on your bathing suit and I'll get the children ready. I heard about a place yesterday that you're going to love."

Love it she did. They drove up their road and parked several miles from the cabin. Following Ryan, they took a short path through the woods to a sandy beach on the Chattooga River. The river was only about thirty feet wide and waist-deep, perfect for swimming. But best of all, it rushed over a smooth, sloping ledge, slick and slippery and ideal for sliding.

Ryan showed them how to climb up the side of the slope with the aid of a rope that he tied to a tree. He walked carefully out to the middle of the ledge and sat down, pushing off with a quick thrust. In a minute the water had carried him over the slippery rock and he landed with a resounding splash in the pool of cold water at the bottom.

Stacey went next, while the children eyed the experience with the caution of youth. Somehow, from the top it looked much steeper, much scarier, but there were eight little eyes trained on Stacey's slender body, plus one set of taunting grown-up eyes. With a sigh she pushed off. Attempting to follow Ryan's path, she slid too far to the middle, and with a shriek she found herself free falling into a pothole in the middle of the slope. She surfaced to the sound of applause.

The water in the pothole was deep enough for her to immerse herself completely, and once her body was sufficiently numb she relished the icy baptism. Climbing out after a few minutes of splashing around, she finished her slide, landing with a plop in the water at Ryan's feet. Her slide was an outstanding success. The older children, led by their uncle, scurried up the slope like mountain goats while Stacey and Christy watched from the water below. One by one they slid down again and again.

They stayed at the rock slide for hours, sliding and picnicking on the sandy shore. Stacey was enchanted. It was a magic place, one that reinforced the belief that people should have a good time whenever possible.

"Has your bad mood eased?" Ryan asked Stacey as they shared the last of the cookies in their picnic lunch. The children were still not tired of the new entertainment and continued to slide while Christy, who had gone down the slope a few times on Ryan's lap, contented herself with napping on a beach towel.

"Considerably," she said cheerfully. It was difficult for Stacey to nurse a grievance. "Thank you."

"Nothing to it," he said. "Any time you need cheering up, I'll be glad to pull another one of nature's miracles out of storage for you."

Stacey, who privately thought that Ryan Cunningham was one of nature's miracles, just smiled.

Her good mood lasted only through dinner. Ryan, attentive and loving with the children, was out the door like a gunshot after the last little body had been tucked into bed. Stacey watched him shoot down the driveway on his way toward Highlands, and she hoped with a vengeance that he would have a flat tire.

The evening stretched in front of her like a prison sentence. Always able to amuse herself before, she could think of nothing amusing to do at all that night. The cabin was equipped with all the latest paraphernalia to assure no boring moments, and Stacey listlessly turned on the television set in the back room, trying to interest herself in the program on the one channel that she could tune in clearly. It was a prime-time soap opera, and after minutes of trying to concentrate, she realized that she still didn't know who the good guys were. She snapped off the TV set and wandered to the bookshelf to see if MyraLou shared her taste in literature.

She did, to the point that there was nothing on the shelf that Stacey hadn't already read except one thick historical novel with women in various states of medieval undress on the cover. Trying to concentrate on the potboiler, Stacey was surprised by the ringing of the telephone.

Ryan had received numerous business calls since they had settled into the cabin, but none of them had come in the evening. This one was not like any of the others. Stacey recognized the name of one of Tallahassee's finest attorneys, and she took the message with a gnawing sense of dread. The man hadn't shared anything with her, but he had made it clear that Ryan had to get in touch with him immediately.

Stacey checked the clock, wondered if she should disturb Ryan at MyraLou's, and then decided against it. Instead she picked up the book, which had fallen open to a particularly juicy scene, closed it, and put it back on the shelf. She wasted the next hour puttering around in the bathroom—washing her hair, doing her nails, and finally, in desperation, scrubbing the already clean bathtub.

She was asleep in the porch swing, dressed in her nightgown and robe, when Ryan finally came home. "Stacey," he whispered in her ear, "no one has waited up for me since I was sixteen and my dad let me have the car for my first date. This is very endearing."

Opening her eyes, she looked up into his smiling face and sighed. "I'm glad you're home." Her eyes closed again.

"Come on, Georgia peach, I'll carry you to bed." Ryan lifted her as if she were weightless and carried her to the screen door. The contact woke her with a start.

"Put me down, Ryan," she spat like a frightened kitten.

Unceremoniously he loosened his hold, and she slid down his body. It seemed to take forever, and when she was finally standing in front of him, she blinked twice, trying to remember why she was standing on the front porch dressed in her nightgown and robe, facing Ryan Cunningham. "Well?" he asked.

The reason came back in a flash. "Your lawyer called, Ryan. He said to have you call as soon as you came back home, no matter how late."

"Why didn't you call me at MyraLou's?" he asked, running his hand distractedly through his curls.

"I hated to disturb whatever it was you were doing there," she said, nose in the air.

"I wouldn't have minded, Stacey. Blueprints are not as important as what my lawyer has to tell me."

"Blueprints?"

"Yes, blueprints. What did you think I was doing over there every night? I've been consulting with MyraLou on some plans for condominiums over in Sapphire Valley. I'm trying to keep them from destroying any more of the environment than they absolutely have to."

"Well, that's not exactly what I thought you meant when you said your evenings were a labor of love." She sniffed, embarrassed at her own evil thoughts.

Ryan's head snapped back and his body shook with laughter. He enclosed Stacey in a bear hug. "Georgia gal, you're one..."

"Of a kind," she finished for him. "Go call your lawyer."

The news was not good. Even from the kitchen where she was making them coffee, Stacey could hear the anger in Ryan's voice, if not the words. When the phone was slammed back into its cradle, she poked her head tentatively into the living room. "Is it safe to come in here?" she asked in a stage whisper.

The look Ryan gave her was so full of misery that all thoughts of treating his telephone behavior lightly disappeared immediately.

"What on earth is wrong, Ryan?" she asked, moving swiftly to his side.

With a glance at the loft overhead, he motioned her to the front porch. "God," he said, "I hope Caroline didn't hear any of that." Stacey slipped up the loft stairs to check on the little girl first and then followed him out to the porch. "She's sleeping soundly," she reassured him. "Do you want to tell me what's wrong, or should I leave you alone?"

He was standing by the porch railing, absentmindedly beating his fist against the supporting beam, and it was some minutes before he answered her. "The children's aunt is suing for their custody. My lawyer says she's going to get it."

Stacy gave a horrified gasp. "But why? They're doing so well with you."

He turned to face her, and in the soft light from the moon and the small lamp burning in the living room, she could see the lines of anguish etched in his face. "Their aunt is an unprincipled woman, with only one interest. She wants to have control of their estate." He leaned on the railing, arms crossed in front of him. "Tom and Janelle were wealthy, and the children had more money left to them than most people will ever see in a lifetime. The money's all tied up, but their Aunt Katherine will find a way to make use of it, I'll guarantee it."

"Why does your lawyer think she'll get custody, then?" Stacey had collapsed onto the porch swing, and it was gently rocking under her.

"Because she's a pillar of the community. Married for years to a little shrimp of a guy who doesn't say boo, she looks, on paper, like a great candidate for guardianship. I don't."

"Ryan, you're wonderful with the kids!"

"Sure—now let's tell that to the judge. You know I'd do anything to keep the kids, short of hiring a hit man, but do you know what my life was like before, Stacey?" He was shaking his head. "The longest I stayed in one place before this tragedy was six weeks. I roamed the country, jetting from site to site, partying when I wasn't working, building a terrific reputation as a real Casanova. Suddenly I say I'm going to settle down and provide a good home for four young children. What judge would believe it was possible?"

"But you've got friends who will testify to how good a parent you are. Margie and Ron, me..." She tried to think of more.

"Stacey, do you realize how taking you on this vacation will look to a judge?" he asked gently, pushing away from the railing to sit in the swing beside her.

She hid her face in her hands, and he put his arm around her shoulders and drew her close. The tears he couldn't cry were streaming down her cheeks. "There must be something you can do, Ryan. Didn't your lawyer have any ideas at all?"

"Yeah." He laughed with no joy. "He told me to find some sweet young thing and marry her quick."

Stacey was aware, as the silence left in the wake of his remark closed in around them, that the inky blackness was unnaturally still. Where were the frogs, the katydids, the crickets? Why weren't the owls hooting? Why was Ryan's answer still reverberating in the quiet night?

With his fingertips on her cheek, Ryan turned her head to his. "I know what you're thinking, Stacey. You know I'm not going to let you do that for me."

She took a shaky deep breath. "Just how many other sweet young things do you know, Ryan?"

The stillness began again. Stacey lost track of time, of feeling. She was in suspended animation...waiting, waiting.

"I know two women who would marry me in a minute," Ryan finally said. "One has been divorced three times and the other sneezes when children walk into the room."

"What about MyraLou?"

"She's the one with the allergies."

"Ryan," Stacey said haltingly, "there are three women who would marry you in a minute. And I'm obviously going to be your best choice for pleasing a judge." She had just proposed to him, and the sheer audacity of it made her hide her head in his shirt sleeve.

Warm fingers came to rest under her chin, and he lifted her head to kiss her with the respectful kiss of one friend for another. "Of course I can't do that," he chided her. "I care too much about you to ruin your life like that."

"But I love the children too," she stammered. And I love you, she thought, but you're too blind to see it. "I can't bear to have them separated from you, living with someone who doesn't love them." And I can't bear the thought of you married to someone else, she added silently.

Ryan stood, leaning against the pillar again as he watched her in the darkness. "Stacey, hasn't anyone ever told you that you can't go through life trying to rescue everybody you think needs you?"

"Is the thought of being married to me so abhorrent, Ryan?" she asked in a small voice.

"Georgia peach, I don't want to ruin your life. You're young, beautiful, and ready for a real marriage. For a husband you love and children of your own." He shook his head. "Children from your own body. Don't deny yourself that pleasure."

She stood up and faced him, tears tracing a path down her face. "Ryan, I can't have children of my own. If I'm going to be a mother, it will have to be to your children. Won't you give me that chance?"

Chapter Seven

Ryan's arms surrounded her, pulling her to rest against his chest. His thumb wiped away the teardrops that had come to rest in the hollow under her dusky eyelashes. When there were no more tears to wipe away, he guided her to the swing and settled her on his lap. My head fits on his shoulder, she thought distractedly. Every part of me fits perfectly someplace.

"Tell me about it, sweetheart," he murmured as he stroked her hair back from her wet cheek. "Tell me what you mean."

She gulped and exhaled a shaky sigh. "Do you really want to hear the details?" she asked uncertainly. "It's a hard story to tell."

"Tell me, Stacey."

She wanted to tell him; she owed it to him. But it was hard to begin. "It was the year I was in the Miss Georgia pageant. I had just finished high school the year before, and I was working at the local bank as a teller. In the evenings, I'd go home and help my parents." She stopped and sighed again, and Ryan began to place tiny, soft kisses in her hair.

"Go on."

"My dad had decided to add a broiler house—you know, chickens—to the farm, and it was a lot more work than anyone had ever thought. The whole family had to pitch in, even more than we ever had before. At the same time, I was involved in all the preparations for the state pageant."

"And..."

"And I was exhausted. I was working full time to save money for college, helping many hours a night at home, and trying to become a beauty queen. I didn't ever rest. I lost lots of weight, which my sponsors thought was great. I developed a fashion-model figure."

"I can't imagine that," he said softly, his fingers squeezing her waist.

"I did. By the time the state pageant came around I was in a daze. Exhausted, frail, sick. Only, I just ignored all the signs and kept going. I'd never been ill before, I didn't even recognize the symptoms. The night of the pageant I went through the motions as if I was a zombie...and I collapsed when it was over."

"Poor Stacey," he whispered in her hair.

"They rushed me to the hospital. By that time I had a high fever, and the next morning they realized I had to have surgery." She lapsed into silence.

"And?"

"And the surgery left me with very little chance of ever conceiving a child," she finished miserably. "If I had gone to a doctor when I first started having problems, they could have taken care of it easily. As it was, I probably ruined my chances of becoming a mother. For the longest time, I could hardly live with myself."

"Poor sweetheart," he said soothingly, gently. "The ultimate irony. All those people out there who can have babies at the drop of a hat and then never pay the slightest attention to them. You come along with your marvelous rapport with kids, and you can't have them yourself.''

"And it was my own fault," she said, shaking her head. "That was the worst part."

"You said you have very little chance of conceiving, Stacey. There is still a possibility then?"

"A small one. There have been advances in microsurgery that could even increase the odds, I guess. There hasn't been any reason to pursue it, so I don't know."

Ryan threaded his fingers through her hair and pulled her head back to look at her. "What do you mean, no reason to pursue it?"

"Don't you see, Ryan? Even if my chances were as high as fifty-fifty, I knew I couldn't do that to a man. How would he feel about me if we tried and tried, and I couldn't give him a child? I decided that I would never get married." She wanted to hide her head again, but Ryan wouldn't let her.

"Stacey MacDonald, this isn't the Dark Ages. Men don't cast away wives because they don't bear them sons. Any man married to you would be the luckiest devil on earth, children or no children." She watched a slow smile light up his face. "But now I get it. You'd marry me because I already have a house full of kids, and you think I could forgive you your inability to bear me any more." He shook his head.

She dropped her eyes, her chin quivering slightly. "I would understand, Ryan, if you didn't want me. You're young enough to want more children."

His hands gripped her shoulders and he shook her hard. Her eyes flew to his face and her mouth dropped open in astonishment. "Stop it right now, and don't be such a little dunce! So you made a mistake once—so what? It shows you're human; I'd be scared to death of you if you weren't."

He shook her again, more gently this time. "Maybe you'll give birth to your own baby someday, Stacey, and maybe you never will, but it doesn't matter to me. You're already the best damn mother I've ever seen, and those kids in there need what you can give them."

Still recovering from his anger, she didn't comprehend the meaning of his words. "Excuse me?" she whispered.

His voice softened. "If you're crazy enough to want to share my life, I'm not crazy enough to turn you down." His mouth moved to cover hers. "I accept your proposal, Georgia gal. I'll be delighted to marry you."

On Stacey's wedding day the sun shone with such abandon that all the relatives who had gathered to witness the ceremony said that it was God's blessing on the young couple. Standing in the small, cluttered bedroom of the old Georgia farmhouse where she had lived nearly all her life, Stacey hoped that her relatives were right.

"Hike up that corner a little, Caroline," Margie motioned to the little girl who was kneeling on the floor placing pins in the wide lace hem of the traditional white wedding gown. "That's better. Stacey, stop fidgeting. I'll never get this right."

"Then I could get married in the sundress I bought, the way I wanted to," Stacey said, rolling her eyes to the ceiling.

"Didn't anyone ever tell you that your wedding is not your own, honey? It's traditional to have it exactly the way you don't want it. That's part of the fun."

Stacey and Ryan had announced to the children the morning after their conversation that Ryan was going to make Stacey their aunt. "That's neat; what's for breakfast?" had been the reply of the children, who thought that Stacey was already part of the family anyway.

Greeted with more enthusiasm was Stacey's announcement that they would be stopping by her parents' farm to introduce Ryan and the kids and to tell them about the wedding. "You mean we get to meet all your brothers and sisters?" had been the joyous response.

The visit had not gone exactly as planned. Upon telling her parents of their intention to go back to Tallahassee and be married by a justice of the peace, there had been a scene that would remain in Stacey's memory for eternity. Ryan had been no help at all. "I told Stacey she should get married here with her family around her, but she wanted a quiet wedding," he said with a choirboy smile.

With hardly a thought spared for Stacey's preferences, the wedding plans had proceeded without her. The one thing that she had insisted on was that the wedding be performed as quickly as possible. The sooner they were married, the better it would look to a judge. Her mother said she could plan it in a week.

With iron will and nine younger MacDonalds helping, Mrs. MacDonald managed to pull together plans for the kind of wedding that she had always dreamed of giving her daughters. Stacey, the third child but the oldest daughter, was the test case for the four sisters who would follow at her heels, and they let her know in no uncertain terms that she had better cooperate.

"I don't mean to sound ungrateful," Stacey apologized to Margie. "I love this dress, and I'm delighted to be married in your wedding gown."

Margie stood back and surveyed her cousin. "You look so lovely. Take it off and I'll finish that little bit of hem that Caroline pinned up."

"Your dress, Grandmother's wedding veil, Mother's rose garden, the children's wild-flower bouquet. What am I doing here anyway?" Stacey's thoughts had been rambling all morning, and Margie gave her an encouraging pat while eyeing the little girl on the floor.

"Caroline, run see if Grandma MacDonald needs your help," Margie told the little girl. She waited until Caroline was gone and then locked the door behind her. "Now tell me, what is going on here? You act as if this is a funeral, not a perfectly lovely wedding. What gives?"

"I can't figure out what I'm doing here," Stacey said in a daze as she stepped out of the wedding dress and thrust it at Margie. "One minute I'm baby-sitting for a bunch of kids in Highlands, North Carolina, and the next minute I'm in Georgia marrying their uncle. I don't even know Ryan Cunningham!"

"Well, what don't you know about him?" Margie asked, pushing Stacey's stiff body into a chair and handing her a folded newspaper to fan herself with.

"I don't know his family. Today was the first time I even knew that his father walks with a cane and his mother wears glasses. For Pete's sake, Margie, today was the first day I ever saw his parents! And I'm marrying him?"

"Go on." Margie bit off a long piece of thread.

"I don't know where he went to school, Margie. What was he like as a kid? Did he go to church? Was he a boy scout? How old was he when he kissed his first girl? I can't marry him without knowing any of that!"

"You'll have your whole lifetime to find out those details, honey." Margie looked up from the hem and smiled. "You know, I don't know if Ron was a boy scout either. I'll have to ask him."

"I can't stand it!"

"Talk about bridal nerves. This must be a classic case. Do you want me to tell Ryan the wedding is off because you haven't seen his merit badges?"

"If I laugh at that, I'm going to become hysterical," Stacey warned Margie. "Don't make me laugh; sympathize with me."

"I'm sorry," Margie said in mock apology. "Here you are marrying the most attractive man in three states, inheriting four lovely children and becoming a wealthy woman to boot, and I can't sympathize with you. Naughty me."

"Wealthy woman?"

"Ryan's loaded, honey. Don't tell me you didn't know?"

"See? I don't know anything. For all I know, he sleeps in a twenty-five-year-old tent in the rain because he has to." Stacey thought about Margie's words. "But you're right, I must be crazy to be so upset. Only..."

"Only?"

"Only, I just wish I knew how Ryan was feeling right now."

As if the entire MacDonald clan were part of a huge conspiracy, Stacey and Ryan had not had two minutes alone since arriving at the farm. When they saw each other, it was always in the company of one or more chaperones. Even walks around the property were conducted by tour guides. Their most intimate moments came at night, just before Stacey joined two of her sisters, Caroline, and Christy in her cramped bedroom. Then Ryan was allowed to give her an obligatory goodnight kiss, properly chaperoned, of course.

From the beginning, Stacey was amazed by the way Ryan fit into her family. Watching him as he sat in a rocking chair on the front porch with her father discussing crops and the world situation, she could not distinguish Ryan from any of the numerous local cronies who often sat in the same spot, discussing the same subjects.

Her mother, at first naturally suspicious of any man who dared to propose to one of her daughters, was completely charmed. She baked and fed peach pies to Ryan as if he were a starving waif from a third-world country. Stacey's brothers took him fishing, her sisters flirted outrageously. Ryan was the hit of the summer. The only person who hadn't gotten to spend any time with him was Stacey.

A pounding on the locked door shook Stacey out of her reverie. Her father's voice sounded from the other side. "Stacey, just about everybody's here. They're going to start the music in a few minutes. You have half an hour to finish dressing."

Margie unlocked the door. "Your sisters are going to want to help you get ready, and the dress is finished. Chin up, girl. It's too late to have second thoughts."

Stacey leaned heavily on her father's arm as she walked up the flower-strewn path to the circle of rose bushes that was her mother's pride and joy. Christy had gone first, toddling solemnly up the aisle throwing rose petals to the wind. Next had come Caroline and Heidi, Margie's oldest daughter. Stacey's four sisters followed and Margie, as matron of honor, brought up the rear. There hadn't been time to create matching dresses, but each female was dressed in her finest party wear. It was a procession magnificent enough for a queen.

Ryan was already at the front with the preacher. Tom Sawyer in a dark suit, Stacey thought wildly. This couldn't really be Ryan. She caught his eye, and he flashed her a broad grin. She relaxed slightly. She might not recognize the suit and the elegant dress shoes, but the grin was all Ryan. She smiled shyly at him. Her father placed her hand in Ryan's and the wedding began.

It was a picture-perfect ceremony, except for one small incident. "Will you take Anastasia Elizabeth to be your lawful wedded wife?" the preacher asked Ryan. Stacey, who hadn't been able to look directly at Ryan during the long ceremony, lifted her eyes during the weighted pause. Ryan was smiling down at her. "Anastasia Elizabeth?" he mouthed before he answered, "I do."

The gold ring Ryan placed on her finger was heavy and handmade. She had been surprised when he insisted on matching bands, but she was delighted now that she saw his choice. When the preacher gave him permission to kiss her, Ryan's kiss was more than an obligatory one, and her relatives and friends burst into applause. The wedding was over.

There were kisses and handshakes and a few tears. The children, dressed in wedding finery, chased each other through the roses, and the adults walked back to the house to begin the elaborate celebration barbecue that had been planned for the afternoon.

Everyone had brought something special to the wedding feast, and although almost everyone there was officially a teetotaler, wedding champagne was exempted from the list of beverages that had to be teetotaled. Food and champagne were abundant, and the preacher turned his head at the latter.

One of Stacey's second cousins played the electric guitar in a country rock band, and he and his band set up their equipment on the front lawn. The older relatives joked that they wished he was a second cousin far removed, but everyone danced, even those who didn't believe in it. Stacey was whirled from partner to partner, finally excusing herself to go inside and change into a strapless white gauze sundress. Ryan had taken off his jacket and tie and rolled up the cuffs of his spotless white shirt. When she emerged, he claimed her as his partner as the band began to play a sensual country ballad.

"Hello," he whispered in her ear as he wrapped his long arms around her waist. "This is the first time in a week that I've been allowed to get this close to you."

Her hazel eyes were wide as he pulled her even closer. "They must approve of you," she said seriously. "With anyone else it would have been our first wedding anniversary before they'd let me dance like this."

"Your family's wonderful," he said in a teasing tone. "After your father gave me the third degree out behind the barn the first night, they've all been very friendly."

"You're kidding!" she said, head pushed back to look at him. "He didn't." She thought for a moment and then sighed. "He did."

"He certainly did. I had to account, in colorful detail, for every moment you and I have spent alone since the first time I saw you."

"You didn't!" Her eyes were as wide as their natural boundaries would permit. "Did you tell him everything?"

"Do you think I'm crazy?" He laughed. "But I assured him of your continued chastity and my constant chivalry."

"What did he say?" she asked, putting her head against Ryan's shoulder again.

"He said that any man who could take one of his beautiful daughters on a vacation for two weeks and remain chivalrous was a model of self-control. Then he welcomed me to the family."

"That's my father," Stacey said with pride.

Ryan's father claimed the next dance. Stacey had been surprised when Ryan's parents dropped everything to come to the impromptu wedding, but she was very happy that Ryan wanted them there. Although she had had almost no time to spend with them since their arrival that hectic morning, she knew from her limited contact with them that they were going to be good in-laws.

"You're a credit to the family, Stacey," Ryan's father said gallantly. Mr. Cunningham, white haired and bent with arthritis, was much older than Stacey had expected, and they were moving very slowly to the music.

"Thank you," she said with a smile. "I've been wanting to tell you that I hope you and Mrs. Cunningham understand why Ryan and I felt we should be married so quickly. I know that you're all still in mourning, and I wish we could have waited."

Mr. Cunningham squeezed her hand. "I understand, and believe me, Janelle would have wanted it this way. Be happy, Stacey. We're happy for you."

In the flurry of congratulations and hugs, Stacey had not had a chance to eat. When she and Ryan finally joined hands to cut the wedding cake, she had to restrain herself from licking the icing off his fingertips. "Why do you have that gleam in your eye, Georgia Brown?" he asked her.

"I'm starving, and you look good enough to eat," she said without thinking.

"Plenty of time for that later," Ryan said with a smile. "But if you're talking about something else, I think I can help."

She sat on a blanket under a huge oak tree, thinking about his words. Ryan had gone to get her a plate of food, and for the first time since she had awakened that morning, she was alone. The anxiety that had been building since the night she had proposed to him finally came out from under cover. At no time in their discussion had they ever touched on the question that was central to her attack of nerves. What was Ryan expecting of her? Was this going to be a real marriage, in every sense of the word, or was it a business deal between interested partners?

The only discussion they had engaged in about their wedding night had revolved around where they should spend it. In deference to the needs of the children, who might feel abandoned if Stacey and Ryan left, they had decided to stay at Stacey's parents' house that night and leave for Florida the next morning with everyone in tow. There had been no mention of a honeymoon, an improbable idea for a couple with four insecure children, and they had both approached their wedding night plans with great practicality.

Stacey's parents had arranged to have her sisters and Caroline and Christy sleep in a screened-in porch at the far end of the house in order to give Stacey and her new husband privacy. The room she and Ryan would share was the room that had been her bedroom for nineteen years, and the thought of the two of them alone in it gave her helpless shivers.

"Here you go." Ryan was back and handing her a heaping plate. "Eat fast—I saw the troops loading up with enough rice to feed India. Since we're not going anywhere tonight, they're going to find us and throw it at us before they leave instead."

Finally, stuffed with food and barraged by rice, Stacey stood on the porch waving as her relatives and friends drove away. Ryan's parents were going to stay with a nearby uncle of Stacey's for the night before they flew back to the retirement village where they lived in southern Florida. Stacey kissed them both good-bye, promising them that she and Ryan and the kids would come and visit as soon as they were finally settled in their new house.

At last they were alone...with only the nine unmarried MacDonald children, Caroline, Christy, David, Jonathan, and Stacey's mother and father to keep them company. There was no help for it; the evening stretched before them with no hope of privacy, no chance to share thoughts, no way to determine what was expected of either of them during the long night ahead.

Now that the wedding was official, Stacey's brothers, especially the fifteen-year-old twins, James and Randy, had declared open season on subtle innuendos. Stacey tried to take their teasing with good humor or pretended ignorance, but the tension was building inside her until, by the time she could gracefully escape to prepare for bed, she was a nervous wreck.

Alone in her room, she sat forlornly on a three-legged stool looking out at the yard below. The moonlight was as bright as the sun had been earlier, and she could see the graceful outlines of her mother's rose garden and the straight tall rows of corn and pole beans in her father's vegetable patch. There was a bright star shining directly over the cow barn, and right behind the little pond in a field close by she could detect the movement of her youngest sister's pony. This was home, but that fact was little comfort. She was no longer Stacey MacDonald. She was married to a stranger now, and this place would never really be home again.

In a trance she rose and showered quickly in the bathroom down the hall from her room, returning to pull out a white silk nightgown that had been a wedding present from Margie. The material clung to her warm, damp body as she pulled it over her head. It was of midthigh length and of impossibly sheer material; the lace-trimmed bodice hugged her breasts while the slit up one side exposed all of her long, shapely leg. "Help!" She gulped as she looked at herself in the mirror.

"That's not what I would say," said a voice from the door, and Stacey turned slowly to see Ryan standing there watching her. "I'd say beautiful."

She blinked twice, forcing herself not to run for cover. Reaching for a hairbrush, she turned back to the mirror and began to undo the pins that had held her hair in French-braided loops under her wedding veil.

"Let me do that," Ryan said, and in a moment he was across the room, standing behind her as she dropped her shaking fingers and shut her eyes. "You hair is so lovely," he murmured. "It falls through my fingers like a silken cobweb." She could feel the last pin being removed and the tumble of her hair to her shoulders. Ryan picked up the brush and began to gently pull it through the shining mass.

"There," he said, and he turned her toward him. "Well, Anastasia Elizabeth," he said in a husky whisper, his index finger tracing a line down the side of her face. "How do you feel about your wedding day?"

If he had substituted night for day, she might have fainted. As it was, all she could answer was, "You didn't even know my real name."

It was a basic symptom of what was wrong between them, she thought as she watched the tender expression on his face. If the serious conversations that they had indulged in were placed end to end, they wouldn't take as much time as a television soft-drink commercial. She and Ryan were strangers. Tom Sawyer and Rebecca of Sunnybrook Farm were married, and he hadn't even known her name.

"It's all right, Anastasia Elizabeth," Ryan said, his beautiful grin making a small dent in her anxiety, "I plan to spend lots of time learning all the important things about you. Beginning tonight."

She wasn't sure she could trust his answer, and it seemed imperative to be sure she understood. She probed. "What kind of things, Ryan?"

"How your skin feels," he said, moving closer to her, "how your eyes look when they're soft with pleasure, and how your smiles changes when you've been satisfied."

There it was. The answer to all her questions, the truth that had sent her body and soul into an endless whirl of uncertainty and doubt. Ryan intended to make their marriage a real one. And glorious truth, amazing response, she was so relieved she could hardly stand up. It was not fear that was making her knees weak now, it was anticipation. This man, her beloved stranger, the person she was learning to love most in the world, wanted to make her his.

Her sisters had thoughtfully pushed two hard single beds together in the corner of the room near the window, and Ryan led Stacey by the hand to the improvised double bed, sitting down and pulling her to stand between his knees. With one hand he unbuttoned his shirt, the fingers of his other hand entwined with hers.

There was no question about it, he obviously sensed the struggle she had just endured, and his response was one of kindness and reassurance. "Do you know, Stacey," he whispered huskily, "that from the first moment I saw you standing in Margie's living room, I wanted you?" He squeezed her hand as a small tremor passed through her body. "Do you have any idea how difficult it's been to keep my hands off you?"

The news wasn't a surprise. Other men had desired her; she had learned at age fifteen that her soft body and pretty face inspired need in a fair percentage of the male population. But knowing that Ryan wanted her sent desire spiraling through her own body. It also effectively tied her tongue. She tried to smile but could manage only a short-lived, one-sided smirk. She hoped that the rest of her body would be more cooperative with Ryan's plans for it.

Shirt unbuttoned, Ryan pulled her close, imprisoning her between his strong thighs. She fit perfectly, a condition that she had come to expect, and she rested her cheek on his dark curls, hands slowly exploring his back. His warm breath was at her breasts, and her excitement at the touch of his hands and lips was visible through the lacy nightgown. How long they remained in that position she couldn't tell, but when Ryan pulled her to his lap, removing his shirt in the process, she was ready for the heat of his embrace.

Watching her skin tinge with color, Ryan slowly untied one strap of the nightgown. When the silky ties fell to her waist, she gasped softly. "It's all right, sweetheart," he reassured her, his fingers not yet claiming the sweet prize that he had uncovered. Instead he stroked his hands through her hair, kissing her as he did so, running his tongue over her lips until she opened her mouth for him.

He repositioned her, settling her comfortably on his lap as he untied the second strap. She couldn't help it—her eyes closed involuntarily as he moved her away momentarily to look at her. "Lord, you're beautiful," he said, in a voice filled with tender awe. "So very, very perfect."

She had been waiting years for that reassurance. Her illness had left her feeling less than a woman, and Ryan's words made her realize how wrong she had been. "Ryan," she whispered, her eyes fluttering open. "Thank you."

Surprised by her response, he brought her to rest against his chest as he stroked her back. Her soft breasts pushed against the hair-roughened muscles of his chest and the sensation was glorious. "The sweetest, most feminine woman I've ever known," he murmured.

Those words were the signal for the beginning of serious lovemaking. Stacey melted into him like salt water taffy on a summer afternoon. Ryan was patient, but she became increasingly glad that his patience was dissolving. His hands moved faster; her body pressed closer; his kisses became more intimate; her heart was given steadfastly into his keeping.

Finally, Ryan pushed her gently to the bed, removing the silky gown from underneath her willing body. She no longer felt awkward; she felt she was his for the taking. And it was at that moment that a noise from the room next door invaded her consciousness.

It was a giggle; she was sure of it. Ryan had stood up to finish undressing, and with a faint, lingering trace of shyness, she had turned her head. Trying to ignore the noise, she turned toward him and a soft gasp escaped her as she saw him standing, magnificently male, in front of her. She heard the noise again. It was definitely a giggle, followed closely by a scraping sound and another giggle.

She had heard those same sounds years before. During Stacey's adolescence, the MacDonald kids had developed an elaborate system for spying on one another. In a house where privacy was impossible anyway, they had discovered methods of making sure that no one kept any secrets. Stacey knew now, as sure as anything, that her twin brothers were firmly rooted to their closet floor, listening for noises from her room with a jelly glass pressed to the wall.

The realization that every sound that she and Ryan made was being duly recorded by two fifteen-year-old boys was like ice water thrown on the heat of Stacey's desire. When the old springs on the bed creaked as Ryan knelt down beside her, she winced, expecting a giggle. She was not disappointed.

Chastising herself for allowing two sex-starved adolescents to distract her, she tried grimly to put her brothers out of her mind. A door slammed somewhere and she could hear her mother's voice drifting up the stairwell. There was the sound of running feet in the hallway, one of the MacDonald dogs began to claw at a nearby bedroom door, and the pipes began to creak as someone ran bath water.

Try as she might, Stacey could not ignore any of it. Suddenly, she felt as though she were making love to Ryan in plain view of the entire universe. Stacey, who had been raised to be modest in the extreme, who had suffered a thousand deaths parading in front of strangers in a bathing suit, was overwhelmed with humiliation.

"What's wrong, Stacey?" Ryan was still, lying on his side next to her and watching the expressions pass across her face.

There was no way she could explain herself to him. Her brothers were listening, she was afraid that she was going to cry, and the sheer naïveté of her response to the noises around her was painfully embarrassing. She was heartsick that her reactions were coming between them. As she lay in bed with her stranger husband, her wall of silence was destroying the sweet rapport that they had found together. Even knowing that, even wanting him so much she ached from it, she still shook her head, unable to speak.

It was inevitable that Ryan would not understand. He stiffened next to her, and the movement brought tears to her eyes. "I gather," he said formally, "you would prefer that I leave you alone."

She could not respond, tears continuing to gather in her eyes at his tone.

"I see," he said. He sat up and bent over to retrieve her nightgown, which he dropped unceremoniously on top of her. "I'm aware now, Stacey, that you didn't expect any of this. I knew you married me for the children; I just didn't realize that that was the only reason." He ran his fingers through his curls. Sitting up in bed, unclothed, he was the most beautiful thing she had ever seen, and the welling tears spilled over onto her cheeks.

"Ryan," she whispered, trying to force herself to explain.

"Go to sleep, Stacey." He lay down on the far edge of the bed, hands under his head. Haltingly she sat up and pulled the rumpled nightgown over her head. "I'm sorry I misunderstood," he said into the darkness. "You can rest assured, it won't happen again."

Chapter Eight

Getting up and going downstairs to breakfast the next morning was the hardest thing Stacey had ever done. Ryan had risen with the roosters, showered, and changed while she remained curled up in bed, pretending to sleep. When she finally opened her eyes he was gone. It was a full hour before she could bring herself to face her family and her new husband.

The kitchen was as empty as the MacDonald kitchen ever got. Her brother Randy, Ryan, and Christy were the only ones still having breakfast. Christy caught sight of her and with her mouth stuffed full of cereal screeched, "Mommy!"

Taking a deep breath, Stacy stepped into the bright, airy room. "Good morning," she said tentatively. "Where is everybody?"

"Good morning, Stacey," Ryan said cordially. "Your mother and father are out checking the chickens, and the kids are riding your sister's pony." With difficulty she met his eyes. His expression was polite but remote. For all practical purposes she was a stranger.

Finding her way by instinct to the refrigerator, she got out milk and orange juice. "Do you need anything, Ryan?" she asked, her voice sounding formal and remote too.

"No, thank you, Stacey." He stood up to get Christy down from her high chair.

"Well, I'll leave you two lovebirds alone," Randy said with a smirk. "I'm sure you have a lot to talk about...now." He sauntered off, trailing a path of toast crumbs behind him.

"Charming, isn't he?" Stacey snapped, anger enlivening her tone. "Teen-age boys should be incarcerated until they're at least twenty."

Ryan was obviously puzzled by her outburst. "Is it all men you dislike this morning, Georgia gal, or only the ones you happen to be related to?"

It was as good a time as any to explain her anger and her behavior of the night before. Swallowing hard, she turned to face him. "Ryan, last night James and Randy..."

"Good morning, honey. Did you sleep well?" Mrs. MacDonald bustled into the kitchen, clapping her hand over her mouth at her own words. "Forget I asked," she said as Stacey blushed.

Stacey stared at her mother. Eldora MacDonald was still an attractive woman in a softly rounded, matronly way. Her golden brown hair was streaked with gray, and her face was wrinkled from laughter and hard work under the blazing Georgia sun. But to her family, and to others who knew her, she was still beautiful. Laughing, she patted Stacey's hand on her way to the stove to replenish the ever-present pot of hot coffee. "Believe it or not, child, I was a newlywed once myself."

Stacey blushed again, refusing to look in Ryan's direction. He surprised her by coming up from behind and leaning over to place a platonic kiss on her cheek. "I'll take Christy out to see the pony while you eat," he said, loudly enough for Mrs. MacDonald to hear. For Stacey's ears alone came the message, "You don't deserve those blushes, you know."

There was no chance to talk to Ryan during the busy morning while they packed their clothes and prepared to leave for Florida. The children complained bitterly about being dragged away from their new aunts and uncles, some of whom weren't much older than they were. Stacey watched James and Randy saying good-bye to David and Jonathan who, after a week in their presence, were taking on some of the older twins' mannerisms.

She sent the younger boys to their seats in the van and then turned on her brothers. "So help me," she said, fire in her eyes, "if you ever, ever try another trick like the one last night, you'll wish you hadn't been born!"

The boys had the grace to squirm under her harsh gaze. There was an instant of startled silence in the flurry of good-byes, and Stacey caught Ryan watching her, puzzled by her behavior. "Stacey?" her mother asked.

"Just a little sisterly advice, Ma," Stacey said virtuously. She turned back to glare at her brothers. "You do understand, don't you, boys?" she asked with syrupy sweetness.

"Yes, Stacey," they chorused.

"And if you dare teach my boys your little tricks," she said so that only they could hear, "nothing I've ever learned about you in your fifteen years of living will be safe with me."

"Yes, Stacey," they chorused again.

"Say good-bye, boys," she prompted them.

"Good-bye, Stacey."

An hour down the road, Stacey realized that the rest of the day was going to be impossible for serious conversation. The children all napped, as she had hoped they would, but they napped on different schedules. There were always little ears listening to the polite conversation that she and Ryan indulged in.

The trip, which had been so much fun when they had been heading north, was no fun in reverse. Instead the hours spent in the van seemed interminable. After a short time on the road, Stacey and Ryan stopped talking at all, each preferring to give up the pretense that they really had anything to talk about.

It was dark when they pulled up in front of Ryan's condominium. "Everybody out," he said tersely. Stacey squeezed between the seats to get Christy out of her car seat and then followed everyone inside.

"It's late, kids," Ryan announced. "Everyone into bed. We can unpack in the morning."

The twins headed for the trundle bed that had been set up in the bedroom they had shared with Ryan. Caroline took Christy into the other bedroom. The question of the day loomed as large as life, but Ryan seemed blissfully unaware of Stacey's problem. "Ryan," she finally asked, "where do you and I sleep?"

The look on his face was unbelieving, and Stacey winced. "I sleep with Jonathan and David, and you sleep with the girls. Under the circumstances that seems to be our best alternative, don't you think?" He gestured impatiently. "Maybe you'd prefer to take the girls back to your own apartment, but for appearances' sake, you should stay here."

She gathered her failing courage. "That's not what I had in mind," she stammered. "I thought possibly..."

"There's no other arrangement I can think of that would benefit either of us. Now, will you go see if the girls are ready to be tucked in? I'll take care of the twins."

It was apparent that it was not the right time to discuss their marital arrangement. Miserably, Stacey turned and walked to the bedroom door. "Stacey."

She turned at the sound of Ryan's voice. "Yes?"

"I'm going to bed myself. I didn't sleep well last night and I'm tired." For a second, his eyes flickered over her, but his interest died quickly. "I'll see you in the morning," he said gruffly and disappeared into his bedroom.

The pattern of the following two weeks was set the next morning. Stacey awoke to the reassuring sound of Ryan's housekeeper, Mrs. Watson, letting herself into the apartment. In a few minutes, the good smell of bacon frying permeated the air. Pulling on a robe, Stacey poked her head out of the bedroom door to say good morning.

"Good morning, Mrs. Cunningham," Mrs. Watson said heartily. "I saw Mr. Cunningham in the parking lot and he told me about your marriage. I'm so happy for you both."

Stacey smiled wryly. "Thank you. Did Ryan say where he was going?"

"Just that he'd be working all day and to tell you that you could reach him through his secretary if you had to."

Stacey and the children spent the day unpacking and, with Mrs. Watson's help, washed and put away clothes. By supper time, Ryan hadn't arrived, finally calling to tell them to go ahead and eat without him. An hour before the children's bedtime, he appeared. After myriad hugs and kisses, he spent the remainder of the evening rough-housing and reading them stories. When they were finally tucked happily into bed, he flopped on the sofa to immerse himself in the newspaper.

"Hard day?" Stacey asked, sitting down beside him.

He seemed mildly annoyed at her question. "Very," he said shortly. "And yours?"

It was a polite response, but Stacey couldn't convince herself that he really cared. "Busy," she answered. "We unpacked and did a general cleaning up."

"Good," he said, holding the newspaper up to his face once more.

She waited until he had finished the front section before she tried again. "Do you think you'll be this busy every day?"

"Probably," he answered, not even bothering to lower the paper.

"I see." And she did. Ryan was making his position perfectly clear. Lower that paper, she pleaded silently with him. Give me a chance to explain, to tell you how I really feel.

When he finished the comics, he read the sports section. Finally he hurled the paper to the glass coffee table in front of him. "What is it, Stacey?" he asked in irritation at her continued presence.

"Ryan," she began tentatively. "We have to talk. I have to explain about last night."

"No explanations are necessary, Stacey," he assured her. "You made yourself understood last night, although I'd love to know why you waited so long to let me know my attentions bothered you."

"It's not what you think," she began.

"What do I think?" he interrupted her.

"Don't badger me, Ryan," she said with a touch of spirit. "I'm trying to explain something to you and it's not easy to do."

He was silent, but his eyes were as cold as a snowstorm.

"Last night, I didn't know, that is, I didn't expect..." Her voice trailed off at the look in his eyes. "You never made it clear to me that you expected anything of me other than being a mother to your kids. If I'd known what you had planned, I'd..."

"You'd have run the other way," he said shortly, standing up and stretching. "Maybe it would have been better for us both if you had, Georgia gal."

He turned and was gone before she could finish her sentence, before she could tell him that if she had known that he wanted her as a real wife, she would have insisted they start their marriage somewhere else, anywhere they could truly have been alone. And his refusal to listen to the words she had almost been able to say left her unwilling to try to say them again. She lifted her chin and wiped away the tears she hadn't even known had fallen. Ryan Cunningham was about to find out that he was not the only person living in the tiny condominium who could be unbearably stubborn.

Their interactions for the next two weeks were stilted and formal. Neither of them made any attempt to spend even five minutes alone in the other's presence. When Ryan arrived, Stacey withdrew; when Stacey had to be present, Ryan found something else to do, somewhere else to go. It was a marriage made in hell.

Exactly two weeks after the cold war had started, Ryan asked Stacey to stay and talk for a few minutes after the children had been tucked into bed. The request, even formally issued, melted the icy barrier that she had erected to shield herself from the pain she was feeling.

Ryan had changed after coming home from work into a favorite khaki shirt and dark brown jeans. He was barefoot, his curls were rumpled, and he was undeniably the sexiest man she had ever seen. The emotional aches of the last two weeks were disappearing in smoke. What was pride worth? she asked herself. Was it worth a lifetime of misery?

Frightened of his animosity but ready to make new overtures, Stacey moved to the sofa to sit beside him. He cocked one eyebrow and there was a ghost of a grin on his face. It was like the sun breaking through after a hard winter's storm. She took a deep breath. "I've missed you," she said simply.

Obviously surprised, he took a long time assessing her sincerity before he answered cautiously, "That's good."

"Have you missed me?" she asked.

"Yes, I've missed you," he said with a real smile. "I've missed my Georgia gal. Living like this is sheer hell." He held out his arm, and she moved under its sheltering circle to lean against his chest.

"It has been awful," she said mournfully. "I've learned ways to avoid you that I didn't know even existed. Once I spent a whole evening cleaning out a closet that didn't even have anything in it, just to stay out of your way."

Ryan was laughing and his arm tightened around her. "I'm sorry, Stacey. I've been acting like an adolescent whose girl friend won't make out in the back seat of his father's Chevrolet. I promise I'll behave."

Ryan behaving was not exactly what she wanted. "I'd like to start all over," she said tentatively. "I'd like us to have a real marriage."

She couldn't see his face, but he seemed to stiffen and she drew back in confusion. "Is that such a bad idea?" she asked shyly.

"I'm not sure what you mean by a real marriage," Ryan answered after a silence, "but I don't want anything you don't really want to give me." Before she could protest he went on. "We both know you married me for the sake of the kids. I have no right to expect any more of you just because I have a piece of paper that says you're my wife."

It was like being on a train going one hundred miles an hour, and there seemed to be no place to get off. The right words, the words that would stop him, wouldn't come.

"But if we're going to live together, let's be friends at least," he finished.

"Ryan," she wailed in exasperation. "I want more from this relationship than someone to play Monopoly with."

If he understood her meaning, he gave no sign of it. "I'm giving you a home, a family, and my companionship. That's actually a lot, when you think about it," he said, settling back and stroking her hair in an infuriatingly friendly manner.

What kind of trick was it that Tom Sawyer was playing now? she wondered. Innocent she might be, but not innocent enough to believe that a man as virile as Ryan Cunningham could be so casual about just being friends with his wife, especially after once admitting that he desired her very much. There had to be a method to his madness, but sitting this close to him, she could not puzzle it out. All she knew was that his warmth, his strength, and his curly hair were driving her to distraction.

"Anyway, that's not why I asked you to stay," he said. "I wanted to ask you for a very large favor."

Anything, she thought. Anything at all. "What?" she asked out loud.

"The farmhouse will be ready to move into next week."

"Thank goodness," she said.

"I've been thinking about furniture, and before we go off and buy anything, I'd like the children to pick out whatever they want from their parents' home and have it shipped here. I'd like you to take them there and help them choose."

"Can we do that without the custody issue being settled?" she asked him. Stacey knew that Janelle's house had been sitting unoccupied and all belongings intact, waiting for the children's permanent guardianship to be determined.

"Their Aunt Katherine has canceled her suit for custody. It seems that our marriage did the trick."

Stacey clapped her hands, and Ryan squeezed her shoulder. "Thanks to you," he said, "the kids are now unequivocally mine."

"Ours," she corrected him. "Unequivocally ours." She smiled to herself. And you, Ryan Cunningham, even if you don't know it yet, are unequivocally mine.

Ryan insisted that Stacey and the children fly to Boca Raton to choose the furniture, and Stacey insisted that she be allowed to drive the van. Ryan next insisted that Stacey take van-driving lessons under his expert tutelage, and Stacey then insisted that since she had been driving her father's ornery pickup for years, she could manage without his lessons. Finally Ryan, hands thrown up in defeat, insisted that Stacey do what she wished, and Stacey, in her friendliest fashion, agreed.

They set off the next morning with mixed emotions. The children, especially Caroline, were anxious about returning to the home they had known with their parents. Stacey was anxious about leaving Ryan all alone to resume his bachelor existence, and Ryan, who promised that he would miss them, didn't seem anxious at all.

After studying the map and making careful calculations, Stacey decided she would spend the first night in St. Petersburg near the retirement community where Ryan's parents lived. They arrived late and checked into a motel on the beach, stopping for a brief swim before calling Mr. and Mrs. Cunningham. The older couple were delighted to see them, and even more delighted when Stacey asked them to keep Christy while she took the other children to Boca Raton.

"We can handle one at a time," Mrs. Cunningham, a woman fast approaching seventy, told Stacey in confidence. "But we just aren't young enough anymore to keep up with all four of them. Thank goodness for Ryan and for you, dear."

The next day's drive went smoothly without Christy, who had seemed quite contented to stay with her grandparents. The children were quiet, obviously thinking about what going home would be like, and Stacey made as few stops as possible.

They pulled into Boca Raton after dark, and Stacey, bleary eyed from two days of driving, was only half aware of palm trees, of neatly kept houses with tile and gravel roofs and yards full of luxuriant foliage. Stopping at a service station, she asked for directions to the house, and as they got closer the children were able to guide her, pointing out the correct turns.

The house was in a well-to-do section of the city, right on the water, and Stacey's first thought was that Ryan had obviously not been the architect. It stood ungracefully at the end of the street, a testament to the worst that money could buy. It was a mixture of styles, a hodgepodge of pillars, windows in all the wrong places, and brick and wood and stone. The house had no intrinsic beauty but instead reflected the zealousness of an amateur who had put everything he liked most into one building with no regard to harmony or design. It was a Frankenstein's monster of architecture, and Stacey loved it immediately.

Inside, it was the same. Furniture had been chosen because each piece had somehow spoken to its purchaser. Almost nothing matched, and if it did, it seemed to have happened by accident. Love and care hung in the air like a tangible force, and Stacey was so overwhelmed by it that she could hardly speak. "Here we are," she finally murmured for lack of anything else to say.

The house had been dusted and aired recently. Stacey knew that Mr. and Mrs. Cunningham had come after the plane crash and packed away all the valuables and most of the mementos so that the children could have them when they were of age. All that was left now was the furniture.

The children were silent; there seemed to be nothing they could say. Stacey cleared her throat. "It's late," she said. "I think we ought to go to bed now, and we can start choosing furniture in the morning."

"I don't want to stay here," Caroline said in a small voice. "I don't want to be here."

"Would you feel better if I slept in your room?" Stacey asked.

Caroline nodded. The two boys could hardly keep their eyes open, and Stacey followed them to their bedroom, helping them prepare for bed while Caroline waited in the hall. Too sleepy to do more than run their fingers over familiar objects, David and Jonathan crawled in between the freshly laid sheets and fell instantly asleep.

"Where's your room?" Stacey asked Caroline. Caroline trudged dejectedly down the hallway to the room at the end. "Here," she said, not touching the closed door. Stacey put her arm around the little girl and opened the door herself, stepping over the threshold with Caroline in tow. "It's lovely," she told the little girl. "Did you pick out the furniture yourself?"

Caroline shook her head but declined to elaborate. Stacey walked around the room admiring the canopy bed and the French provincial dresser and chest of drawers. "I'll bet you want to take all of this back to Tallahassee with you."

"No." Caroline still hadn't touched anything or even gone to sit on her bed.

Stacey tried the straightforward approach. "Why not?"

Caroline shook her head. "Because."

Stacey was surprised by the anger in the little girl's voice, and for a moment she thought it was directed at her. "I'm sorry, Caroline. I shouldn't pry. Forgive me?"

"I'm not mad at you."

Stacey was surprised again. "You look very angry at somebody, sweetheart. Who are you angry at?"

"Them!" Caroline exploded. "My stupid mom and dad." And then the tears began.

Every feeling that had been bottled up, every tear that had never been allowed to fall, came pouring out of the little girl as Stacey sat with her on the big canopy bed, stroking her hair. "I hate them; they went off and left us and then they never came back. If they loved us, they would never have gone in the first place."

"Go on, honey," Stacey murmured, soothing her.

"You're not supposed to hate dead people, but I do!"

"Being very angry and hating somebody are different," Stacey pointed out when the tears began to subside a little. "I think you hate what happened. You don't really hate your parents."

Caroline rested her head against Stacey's shoulder and sniffed. "I feel bad about hating them," she said tentatively. "I used to love them."

"Of course you did, honey. And they loved you."

"But they left us," Caroline wailed.

"Tell me, sweetheart," Stacey said after the storm subsided once more, "when you lived here, did you ever spend the night with your friends or go to slumber parties?"

The little girl nodded. Stacey went on. "And did you ever go to summer camp?"

Caroline shook her head, "But Mommy promised me that I could go this summer." Her chin trembled, and Stacey gave her an encouraging squeeze.

"Did you still love your parents, even when you went to those slumber parties?"

Caroline nodded. "Sure."

"Well, why did you go, then?"

"I liked being with my friends. Sometimes you get tired of being at home all the time."

Stacey let the child's own words sink in. "But I always came back!" Caroline objected to her own logic.

"Caroline, do you really think, in your heart of hearts, that your mommy and daddy didn't want to come home to you?"

The little girl began to sob brokenly again. "They must have been so scared for us," she whispered finally. "They must have been so scared."

Tears slipped down Stacey's cheeks too. "Caroline, I'm going to tell you something that you're big enough to hear but that no one has thought to tell you before.

The plane crash occurred at night. There's every reason to believe that your parents were never aware of what happened to them, that they were sleeping. They never had a chance to be scared, sweetheart. They were together, they had their arms around each other when they died. They knew they were coming home to you and they were happy.''

It was a long time before Stacey and Caroline slept. When all the tears had been cried, when all the anger and the pain had been talked through, Caroline lay down beside Stacey and reached for her hand. ''Aunt Stacey,'' she whispered, ''would my mommy mind very much if she knew that I loved you and Uncle Ryan now?''

''Caroline,'' Stacey whispered back as she squeezed the little girl's hand, ''your mommy and daddy will always have the most special place in your heart. But I can promise you that they would never want you to feel bad about loving anyone else.''

''I think you're right.'' The little girl sighed. ''Mommy always said that love was to share.'' Her last words trailed off as she fell into exhausted sleep.

Stacey lay awake for a long time listening to Caroline's even breathing, and she wondered if it was possible for one person to contain as much love as she felt for Ryan Cunningham and his nieces and nephews. My husband, she thought. And a soft presence, a feeling of warmth passed over her. My children, she thought, and she knew that somewhere, from another world, a blessing had been given.

Chapter Nine

Look what I found, Aunt Stacey." Caroline was seated on a dark blue rug in the living room of the house in Boca Raton, investigating the contents of an antique rolltop desk. "Pictures!"

Stacey flopped down beside her, motioning for David and Jonathan to join them too. "Your grandmother thought she had gotten all the photographs. She told me that she's putting them into albums for each of you to keep."

"She just didn't know where to look for these. I think they're the ones that Mommy never got around to putting in a book. Look at this...."

Stacey took the eight-by-ten photograph out of the little girl's hand. "Oh, I'll bet she was going to frame this," she said softly. It was an informal family portrait done by a professional photographer who had managed to catch them all at their best moment. Stacey examined the picture carefully. The children's parents were smiling at each other, obviously thrilled to be together with their family for the picture. The photograph, like everything else that Stacey had come across in the house, spoke strongly of the warmth and acceptance that the children had known there.

"Everyone looks so happy," Caroline said wistfully. "Do you think we could frame this and put it on the wall at our new house?"

"I think that's a terrific idea," Stacey answered enthusiastically. "Maybe we can find some other photographs to hang too." The four of them rummaged through the drawers, coming up with several more that would be perfect for framing. One was of Janelle and Tom, arms around each other like young lovers. "Your parents were very much in love," Stacey commented. "In every picture I've seen, they look so happy together."

"They were always kissing," David said, remembering. "Not like you and Uncle Ryan."

Out of the mouths of babes, Stacey thought. Obviously the children were aware of the lack of warmth in their uncle and aunt's marriage. With as light a touch as she could manage, Stacey responded, "Well, we haven't been married as long as your folks were. You'll have to give us time."

Everywhere she looked that day as she and the children went from room to room tagging furniture to ship to Tallahassee, she saw tangible messages of the kind of marriage that she desperately wanted to have with Ryan. Nowhere was the love that had existed in their home more obvious than in Janelle and Tom's bedroom.

There was a king-sized bed in the middle of the floor, covered with a rich plush bedspread and pillows. The room had a fireplace, the only room in the house that did, and a bathroom with a Jacuzzi big enough to swim in. There were tastefully done works of art that made Stacey blush, and in the bathroom was a statue that she felt the children should not see.

It was a room to love in, a room to give and experience pleasure in; it was a testament to the joy that the couple had found in their marriage. This is what's missing from my life, Stacey thought as she sat on the edge of the big bed and looked around the room. Without thinking, she stroked the furry bedspread with the tips of her slender fingers. She and Ryan had married, not out of love for each other but out of love for the children. True, she loved him, but never, at any time, had he expressed love for her. Desire, yes, but never love.

"From desire, perhaps love will grow," she murmured to herself. Somehow she had to make Ryan understand that she wanted him, that she needed him. Love took time, but she had time. Ryan might not come to care for her for years, but she had years. If someday she could look around a room like this and know that it was a haven from the world, a place where she and the man she loved could be their happiest, then the years of waiting would be worth it.

The misery and confusion of their wedding night was not irrevocable. Ryan might pretend that he only wanted to be her friend, but the huge mirror on the wall opposite the bed convinced Stacey that her charms had not diminished since her wedding night two and a half weeks before. She ran her hands through her sunny hair, lifting it on top of her head. The innocent, all-American face that stared back at her was faintly discouraging but no different than it had ever been. If Ryan had wanted her before, he must still want her, at least a little.

Perhaps he was playing hard to get...a bona fide Tom Sawyer trick. If I play hard to get too, she reasoned, neither of us will ever get anything. The time to be direct and candid, to explain her behavior during their wedding night, had arrived. Resolutely she pounded her fist on the soft mattress. As soon as she could, she would confront Ryan. She had the resolve; now all she needed was the courage.

She stood up, her eye catching a lovely watercolor on the wall by the door. It showed a young couple in a passionate embrace, against a background of whirling clouds of mist and rainbow colors. Chin in the air, Stacey tagged the picture to be shipped to Tallahassee. "For us, Ryan," she whispered. "For us."

The trip north, back to Tallahassee, took a day longer than the trip south to Boca Raton had. Relieved of their pent-up anxieties, the children wanted to stop and see everything they passed by. Every souvenir shop, every roadside attraction was an excuse to beg for a chance to get out and stretch their legs. They picked up Christy at her grandparents late the first night, and because they were all so tired from the stop-and-go traveling, they stayed in St. Petersburg the next day to sight-see and visit.

Stacey showed Mrs. Cunningham the photographs she was going to frame, and Mrs. Cunningham immediately pulled out another box of pictures for Stacey to choose from. When she and the children started out for Tallahassee the next morning, Stacey was armed with photographs of Ryan as a child, a teenager, and a college student. By far her favorite was the one of him at age twelve, straw hat on curly head and jeans rolled up to his knees—he was starring in his sixth-grade production of *Tom Sawyer*.

Ryan's car was not there when they pulled into the condominium parking lot late in the afternoon. A small moving van was. "What's going on?" Stacey called from the doorway.

Mrs. Watson, wiping her hands on a towel, came out of the kitchen. "Oh, Mr. Cunningham didn't think you'd be back so early. He wanted to surprise you."

"I'm surprised, but I don't know by what," Stacey said, bewildered by the sight of two burly moving men carrying the furniture out of Ryan's bedroom.

A happy child's shriek behind her and the advance of the moving men toward the door caused Stacey to step backward, right into a pair of familiar strong arms. "Welcome home," Ryan's husky voice buzzed in her ear.

Stacey leaned back, pressing her body against his. She crossed her arms against her chest, stroking his arms with her fingertips. "Well, hello," she murmured. "You're just in time to tell me what's going on."

Ryan's body weight shifted and she could feel him turning her to face him. If he was expecting a conversation, she was going to surprise him. The welcome sight of the brown curls tumbling over his forehead and the deep mahogany of his eyes gave her courage to put her plan into action. Standing on tiptoe, she rested her hands on his shoulders and pressed her mouth to his. She had no intention of making the kiss a casual one; she dredged up every bit of information that she had ever gleaned from reading romances and kissing Ryan previously. The kiss might not be a perfect ten, but it was close.

"Why don't you tell *me* what's going on?" he said as she stood in front of him, watching his reaction. His thumbs were caressing the soft skin at her waist, exposed by the plaid blouse tied in a knot at her midriff. Ryan looked like a man on the edge of a discovery.

"I just wanted you to know that I missed you," she whispered. "And I wanted to find out if you missed me."

"And?"

"I think I need more information," she said with a smile, standing on tiptoe to kiss him again.

"Lady, it's really hard to move furniture with you in the doorway," said one of the long-suffering moving men.

"Yeah, but it's not every day we get to see such a good show," the other chided his partner. "Leave the nice couple alone, Ralph."

"It's all right, fellows." Ryan nodded at them. "The lady and I can conduct business elsewhere." He pulled

Stacey by the hand to stand under a live oak tree close by the sidewalk. From the corner of her eye, Stacey saw the children watching the moving men in fascination. She and Ryan were being given a few moments alone.

"Where were we?" Ryan asked her.

"Well, I'll answer your question first," she said, hands on his shoulders to keep him close. "I think you missed me, a little at least. Now it's your turn. What's going on?"

"The farmhouse is livable, finally. We're moving today."

"But Ryan," she worried out loud, "we don't even have any furniture yet, except the little that we're moving from the apartment. The furniture from Boca Raton won't be here for three weeks."

"I know, but these guys weren't going to be available again for another ten days or so, and I thought you'd rather make do at the house than here."

"I haven't even seen the house," she told him. "You'd have to be the best judge of that."

Her statement was a reminder of how unusual their relationship was. Even though they had lived together as husband and wife for several weeks, Ryan had not thought to show her the house that would be her new home, and Stacey had been too proud to ask.

Ryan pushed a lock of hair behind her ear, tracing a line around the edge of her earlobe thoughtfully. "This marriage hasn't been much of a bargain for you, has it, Georgia gal?"

She smiled shyly. "It was the best decision I ever made, Florida boy. Don't ever think otherwise."

He gathered her against him, his hands moving under the shirt to stroke her back, his mouth planting gentle kisses on her forehead. "Are we going to try and make it work, Stacey?" he finally murmured in her hair.

She circled his lean waist with her arms, clasping her hands behind him. "Oh, Ryan. That's what I want most in the world." And standing close to him, her head pillowed on his chest, she had a definite feeling that Ryan wanted the same thing.

That flash of hope stayed with her for the next hour. Ryan had done most of the packing, with Mrs. Watson's help, and the Finlaws had gone to the new house to oversee the unpacking of the first load of boxes and the setting up of the necessities. When the last piece of furniture was wedged tightly into the van, they drove through the Tallahassee streets, picking up a country road that would take them north of town.

"I feel like a kid on Christmas morning," Stacey bubbled, unable to keep her excitement in check.

"You'll like the house. Margie and Ron picked it out, actually. They brought me to see it with the realtor, contract in hand. I saw it and bought it in the space of half an hour."

"Why is it so special?"

"It's spacious, and it was handcrafted with care. I guess, best of all, nobody had touched it in years, so there was no major damage to undo. We just had to go in and repair the ravages of the years, not the ravages of untalented do-it-yourselfers." Ryan turned off the blacktop onto a winding gravel road. Stacey recognized the general area as being very close to the Finlaws' house.

When she thought she could not stand the suspense any longer, they turned in at a driveway marked by a rural mailbox large enough to put Christy in. They passed an acre stand of pecan trees, untrimmed and uncared for but with the promise of a rich crop when restored to health. The driveway dipped through woods tangled with vines and scrub brush. To the left, Stacey could see a pasture tall with scraggly weeds but with the potential for rich grazing land.

They reached the end of the road, and Stacey sat and stared at the house before her. It was a Victorian design, painted a warm yellow with brick-red trim. A wide circular porch wrapped around the house as far as she could see, and it was outlined with ornate gingerbread. The most interesting detail, the eye-catcher that made the house unique, was a round tower on the side away from the driveway. It was a fairy-tale house.

"Ryan, it's wonderful," Stacey cried, clapping her hands. "What a fantastic place!"

"I'm glad it meets with your approval. Come inside when you're ready."

The moving men had come, unloaded, and gone by the time Stacey pulled herself away from her minute inspection of the house's exterior and immediate grounds. She had already decided where to plant her garden and what flowers to put in the flower bed by the time she stepped into the living room.

The house had been lovingly restored. The pine floors had been stripped and finished in their natural tones; the walls had been replastered and the woodwork had been refinished. Ryan pointed out details of the restoration to her as they walked through the first floor.

"I thought about restoring the kitchen for you, Stacey. You're such an old-fashioned girl, I thought you might like to cook on a wood stove and haul water," he teased. Instead, he had installed the most modern appliances, but in such a way that they faded into the background, leaving the original pine cupboards as the focal point of attention.

The one room that was new was an addition at the back of the house. "This used to be a screened porch," he told Stacey, "but it was collapsing. I had it torn down and designed this addition." The new room was a game room for the children; it had windows wrapped around three sides and a free-standing fireplace in the corner.

"This room is just like the one in the cabin in North Carolina," Stacey commented wistfully. "I'll always remember that view of Whiteside Mountain when I come out here."

Ryan put his arm around her and pulled her to stand next to him. It was a casual gesture, brotherly almost, but she shivered at his closeness. "You're such a romantic," he scolded her. "I've never met anyone quite so sentimental."

"You have no idea of just how romantic I can be," she responded, pressing her curving hip against him.

Ryan moved away, just far enough to get a clear view of her face. He lifted a skeptical eyebrow. "All these hints, Georgia Brown. Are you trying to tell me something?"

"Show me the upstairs," she said, trying to meet his eyes directly. "I'd like to see the bedrooms."

The children were already in their rooms when she followed Ryan up the wooden staircase. "This is Christy's room," Ryan said, flinging open the door to the first room at the head of the stairs. The little girl's crib was the only piece of furniture in the room, but the walls had been painted a deep rose color with white trim, and Stacey was enthusiastic about decorating it.

They moved down the hall and looked into the next room. "The boys said they'd like to room together, so I put them in here; it's one of the larger bedrooms," Ryan explained as she admired the way the built-in bookshelves and cabinets had been used to divide the room, giving each brother some privacy.

Then came Caroline's room. It was the tower room and perfect for her. "Your furniture will look beautiful in here," Stacey told the little girl, who was sitting on a temporary cot in the middle of the round floor, Christy by her side. "It's a room for a princess."

Across the hall was the smallest bedroom Stacey had seen yet. Ryan told her it was a guest room. There were only two rooms left, and Stacey held her breath as Ryan opened the next door. "This is my room," he said with no expression. Stacey took in his words. Had she understood his meaning? The room contained all of Ryan's bedroom furniture: a heavy mahogany king-sized bed, matching bureau and dresser, and an outsized drafting table.

"It's very nice," she said uncertainly.

"Let me show you your room." Stacey lifted her eyes to meet his. "It's beside the bathroom, right across from Christy's."

The rest of the afternoon and evening passed in a dull haze. Margie and Ron, with their kids, arrived bringing casseroles and salads for dinner. Margie helped Stacey make beds and unpack pajamas. Stacey responded when spoken to, smiled when something funny was said, and broke awkward silences when she noticed them. Still, when she stood on the front porch waving good-bye, she couldn't remember a thing about the day beyond the point where Ryan had shown her to her bedroom. Her bedroom, a separate place to sleep, a space for privacy, a luxury she didn't want.

"Bedtime," she told the children, herding them upstairs to the bathroom to prepare for bed. Christy refused to climb the steps by herself, and Stacey carried the little girl, then dressed her for bed and read her a favorite bedtime story. The child's clinginess was a distraction, and after Stacey had tucked her into bed and settled the other children, she was aware that a long evening and night were in front of her.

Trudging down the staircase, she found Ryan in the living room unpacking a box of books. "The children would like you to tuck them in," she informed him.

"Stay here, please," Ryan said as he left to say his good-nights. "I'd like to talk to you."

There was no furniture in the room to sit on. Ryan had left his fragile living room suite in the condominium for the new owners. Stacey sat on the floor in the corner on a pillow, hugging her knees with her hands. The room would be lovely when it was furnished and decorated.

There was a fireplace with imported tile and a carved wood mantel flanked by built-in bookshelves. That night, though, Stacey only noted the details. She found no pleasure in them.

"Everyone except Christy was already asleep," said Ryan's voice from the doorway.

Stacey examined him as he stood watching her. We're taking each other's measure like two characters in a prizefight, she thought sadly. We're strangers, and we always will be. She broke the long silence. "What do you want to talk about, Ryan? Suddenly I'm very tired."

"You do look beat. Maybe we should wait."

I'm beat, but not the way you mean, she thought. "Go ahead; what you have to say should be out in the open," she said evenly.

He came over to her corner, dragging a pillow and settling it beside her. "I've got to know if I've made a mistake."

"Go on."

"When I showed you your room, you looked surprised and not at all pleased. What were you expecting?"

She was too tired to feel shy, too upset to be cautious. She watched him for a minute, noting the unbuttoned brown shirt, the well-muscled chest, the sleek way his body fit into the shorts he wore. She took in the clean, sturdy lines of his bare feet. The body of a stranger. Finally she shut her eyes and leaned against the wall. "I expected a marriage. Instead I find that I've been relegated to governess again."

"If you wanted a marriage, you had a funny way of showing me," Ryan exploded angrily. "You froze as solid as a glacier when I tried to make love to you."

Stacey's eyes flew open. "Well, well," she said nastily, "so the serene Mr. Cunningham is still bothered by that."

"Hell, yes, I'm bothered, but I can live with it. Just don't expect me to put you in my bed." He ran his fin-

gers through his curls. "I'm just a man, Stacey. I couldn't
sleep next to your nubile young body every night without taking you in my arms and loving you. I've never
forced myself on a woman, and I don't intend to start
with you just because we're married!"

"You're as blind as a bat, Ryan Cunningham, if you
think that it would take force!" The words echoed off the
walls of the empty room.

"And what would it take?" he asked her finally.

"You're the one with the experience," she shot back.
"How should I know? But I should think that a little
patience and sensitivity would go a long way toward
solving our problem." She stood up. "I'm going to bed.
Good night."

She was half way to the stairs before he caught up with
her. "What do you mean, 'good night'? You're not
walking out on me now, Stacey. We're going to finish this
once and for all."

"What do you want to finish, Ryan?" she half whispered. "We've already said more than we should have."

"I wasn't thinking about having a conversation."
Pressing her to the wall, he moved his body against hers,
and as she gasped he covered her mouth with his, his
tongue exploring the even edge of her teeth. Breaking
free, he groaned. "Damn it, Stacey. I want you. If you
really want me, then we don't have any problems at all."
Suddenly he was everywhere, an all-invasive male taking
her sweetness and turning it into hot, honeyed desire. He
couldn't get enough of her, his hands couldn't touch
enough, his lips couldn't caress enough.

Stacey couldn't respond enough, pressing her body to
his, opening her mouth for more of his drugging kisses,
gasping softly as each new intimacy unfolded. This was
not the sweet seduction of her senses that had been so
moving on their wedding night. This was need, raw and
powerful and frightening. Yet Stacey knew instinctively

that for those few minutes when she would most need his patience and his gentleness, they would be there for her.

"Georgia peach," Ryan growled, "I'm going to carry you up those stairs and make love to you in our bedroom. If you have any doubts, stop me now. It's going to be too late in a minute."

She shivered as his hand cupped her breast, teasing the sensitive nipple. His other hand was exploring the uncharted territory of her willing body, and again she shivered violently against him. "You're not giving me a chance to think...and that's just fine with me."

With a fluid motion, Ryan scooped her up and began to climb the stairway. He pushed the bedroom door open and carried her to the bed. With her arms around his neck, she pulled him down, his chest pushing into her soft breasts. Her fingers laced through the dark curls, feeling their silky texture. Hungrily he was exploring her face and neck with his tongue, one hand deftly unbuttoning the front of her blouse, unhooking the front clasp of her bra. His mouth followed the path of his hand, coming to rest at the rosy tip of her breast. He pulled gently with his teeth, and the unexpected pleasure made her squirm beneath him.

"Do you like that, Georgia gal?" he asked her. "You move under me so sweetly." His mouth descended again, this time to the other breast, and she writhed against him once more.

"That's right, sweet Stacey. Just like that. It's going to be good between us. I promise you."

The sensations whirling through her body threatened to engulf her. His mouth was everywhere, exploring and teasing her softness until she felt she had lost herself completely.

As he unsnapped her shorts and began to slip them off, she opened her eyes for just a moment and they focused on the open door. "Ryan, we forgot the door," she said dazedly.

As he strode across the room to shut and lock it she heard a faint sound from across the hall.

Groaning, she hid her face in the pillow.

"What's wrong?" he demanded.

"Ryan," she groaned again. "Did you hear that?" She concentrated on listening for the sound, and she failed to take in the stiffening of his body. "There, I heard it again. It sounds like Christy." She swung her feet to the floor, pulling her blouse around her, and moved to stand beside him. "It sounds as if she's crying."

"She'll be fine." Ryan's voice was harsh, and Stacey looked up in wounded surprise. She hadn't expected the anger and the distrust that was reflected in his eyes.

"Suppose something's wrong?" she pleaded softly.

"It's a strange house; she's probably just feeling lonely. If you leave her alone, she'll go back to sleep." His voice was like granite, and Stacey leaned against him, running her fingers over his face to soften the hard expression there.

"I don't want to leave you now, Ryan. Please believe me. Just let me check on her quickly. Then I'll feel more comfortable."

"As you wish, Stacey." He jerked away from her. "Only stop playing this game with me, please."

"It's not a game," she cried, hurt by his tone.

"Stop kidding yourself, Georgia gal. You don't want to make love to me—any excuse sets you running as far away as your pretty little feet will carry you. You keep trying only because you know you're supposed to, and Stacey MacDonald Cunningham always does what she's supposed to do."

She tried to reach him but he held her firmly away, his fingers biting into her shoulders. "You can stop worrying right now. I can live without your attentions," he said, thrusting her to one side as he pushed through the door. She heard angry footsteps on the stairs he had so recently carried her up. In shock, she heard the front door slam and, a minute later, the sound of an engine.

It seemed like a century before she could make her frozen fingers button her blouse. Finally she slipped across the hall to Christy's bedroom. "What is it, honey?" she asked, although the words came only by rote.

The little girl was crying quietly, and Stacey, stroking her forehead, was surprised at how warm she felt. "Come on, Christy, let's check your temperature."

An hour later the little girl had been tucked back into bed, her fever under control. Stacey stood looking at the curly hair, the flushed face. Christy had needed her tonight. Coming to her had not been an excuse; in fact, leaving Ryan to see to the child's needs was the hardest thing Stacey had ever had to do. He could have waited, she thought sadly. He could have understood. She left the door open and crossed the hall to her own bedroom, leaving that door open too in case Christy called for her again.

With the bedroom door open, she could hear every small sound in the big, empty house. The only sound she didn't hear that night was Ryan's car. When morning dawned, Ryan still had not returned.

Chapter Ten

Christy woke from a fretful night's sleep running a slight fever again. Stacey waited as long as she felt comfortable and finally called Margie to get her pediatrician's phone number.

"I'm surprised Ryan didn't remember it," Margie said with a laugh. "He called the poor man every time one of the children sighed that first month they came to live with him."

"Ryan's not home," Stacey said shortly. When Ryan had not come home by late morning, Stacey finally gave up hope that he would come back at all and, taking the bull by the horns, she had called him at his office. His very efficient secretary informed her that Mr. Cunningham had asked that nobody disturb him. But Stacey wasn't about to give Margie the details. "I can't get in touch with him."

"Don't worry about Christy. I'll bet it's just a little virus."

Margie was right. After Stacey and the four children sat for an hour and a half in the pediatrician's waiting room, the doctor examined Christy and reassured Stacey that all she had was a sore throat. "She's cutting teeth too," he said, blowing up a balloon for the little girl. "She'll probably be fussy for a day or so, but she's fine."

As a thank-you treat for the four bored children, Stacey stopped and bought them ice cream cones on the way out of town. Ryan's car was not in the driveway when they pulled up to the new house, but a note on the dining room table announced his arrival and departure.

Stacey read it, then crumpled the paper and hurled it into an empty kitchen drawer. Ryan had gone on a surprise business trip and had no idea when he would return. There was an emergency number given, with "Emergency" underlined, and a promise that he would call every night and talk to the children. "Children" was not underlined, but it might as well have been. He had weighted the note with a handful of charge cards, and he had informed Stacey that she could use them to buy any furniture she wished.

She dropped the cards into the kitchen drawer too, determined not to buy so much as a fly swatter for the house without his help. I'm not going to live like this, she told herself. I'm not going to be this man's servant, his babysitter, his girl Friday. I'm going to be his partner, his confidante, his lover. Picking out furniture is just one of the things we are going to do together.

Throughout the long night after he had left, she had come to understand Ryan's feelings. He still wasn't aware of the circumstances of their wedding night, and to him, her concern for Christy was just another in what he saw as a series of poor excuses to avoid lovemaking. Telling him she wanted him and then withdrawing at the last moment, for whatever reason, was to him tantamount to being a tease. Each interrupted love scene was driving him so far away that the odds against him finding his way back to her would have staggered Jimmy the Greek.

She was irritated that he would distrust her desire for him; she was angry that he would walk out on her and spend the night elsewhere; she was unbearably hurt at the thought that he might have sought comfort from another woman after he left her. But she still loved him, and she understood.

We won't have many more chances though, she thought sadly. Too many angry scenes, too much pain, and their marriage could go up in smoke. Come back, Ryan, she pleaded silently. Let's straighten it out together, before we destroy it completely.

The best part of the week went by before Stacey found her way to Margie's house for counseling.

"I wondered when you'd finally come," Margie said, patting her hand. They were sitting at the kitchen table drinking cup after cup of black coffee, and Stacey had been waiting for the extra caffeine in her system to take charge. But nothing seemed strong enough to wipe away the depression she felt.

"How did you know?" she asked Margie, her fingers unconsciously pleating the blue calico tablecloth.

"Well, a happy man doesn't leave his beautiful bride to go off on a long business trip. It's pretty obvious that something is wrong."

Little by little Stacey told the story, almost choking on the intimate details but managing somehow to give Margie the picture.

"They had glasses up to the wall?" Margie cried, shaking her head. "Those twin sex maniacs!"

Stacey, warmed by Margie's comforting words, dragged through the rest of the story. Margie passed her a paper napkin at the end.

"Well, I'd say you have problems, kiddo," she agreed. "Now, stop wallowing in self-pity and get busy and do something about it."

"I don't know what to do," Stacey said miserably. "I feel as if it's out of my hands."

"Have you talked to him since he left?"

"One night I answered the phone when he called the children. He wasn't even polite to me."

"Boy, he's got a bad case."

Stacey forgot to be miserable. "A bad case of what?"

"Love sickness. The poor man doesn't know what's hit him."

Stacey sat stunned by Margie's words. "What are you talking about? Ryan has never at any time pretended to be in love with me. Maybe it will come eventually if we can get through this, but…"

"Oh, stop, Stacey. Enough of this nonsense. The man is head over heels for you. When you walk through a room, his eyes follow you everywhere. He doesn't hear what's said to him, he fidgets, he runs his fingers through his hair. He's so hungry for you he can't see straight."

"Hungry? Maybe…. In love, no," Stacey said sorrowfully.

"Look, honey, I'm going to have to be the one to tell you the facts of life." Margie leaned forward and pulled the tablecloth out of Stacey's clenched fingers. "Listen carefully. Ryan Cunningham could have any woman he wanted…and, in fact, he has. Women fling themselves at his bare feet. Ex-lovers threaten suicide, potential lovers make fools of themselves. Then you come along and all of a sudden, here's a woman who treats him like a regular human being. You don't fall at his feet, you don't climb into bed with him, you look at him with those innocent hazel eyes, and he's so crazy he can't see straight."

"You're the one who's crazy, Margie."

"No—now listen. You're a lovely woman, Stacey, but there are lovelier ones. You're sweet, but there are sweeter ones. You're not Ryan's usual type; you aren't sophisticated; you're so innocent that you're a candidate for human sacrifice.''

"Thanks loads," Stacey said acidly. "I really needed to hear all these compliments."

"The point is, honey, that Ryan is blindly in love with you. He doesn't see that you're just a woman, with faults like everyone else. He sees you through the eyes of love. If it was just desire, do you think you could upset him so?''

"I don't know." Stacey shook her head. "I just don't know."

"I do. Ryan may not know it, you may not know it, but the pair of you are painfully obvious to the rest of us. Wake up; grow up, Stacey. The time has come.''

Stacey let Margie's words settle over her. "Wouldn't it be terrific if you were right?" She sighed. "I wish I knew."

"Can you afford to take a chance?"

"What do you mean?" Stacey looked up to see Margie shaking her tousled head.

"Only this. If you don't move in on Ryan, right now, and prove that you want him, you may not have another opportunity."

"He wouldn't leave me," Stacey said, eyes wide. "He knows the children need me."

"No, but the time to establish real intimacy with your husband is now. And if you miss it now, it may never come again. Go for it, honey." Margie patted her hand. "You can do it."

When the phone rang that evening, Stacey made sure that she was the one who answered it. "I'm going to talk to Uncle Ryan first, and then I'll put you on," she told the children in the no-nonsense voice they had come to know well.

With her heart in her throat, Stacey picked up the receiver. "Hello, Ryan. Yes, they're here, but I wanted to talk to you first." She sighed at the long silence on the other end and then plunged on. "I was wondering if you knew when you were going to be coming home." She held the receiver away from her ear, expecting abuse, but his familiar husky voice was civil.

"I don't know—probably Friday."

"Oh, good," she responded. "I'd like to be able to count on that if I could. I have a surprise for you." Her last words were almost indistinguishable. In her nervousness her accent had become so thick that even she could barely understand it.

The silence was so long that Stacey was sure the phone had malfunctioned. Finally Ryan answered, "All right. I'll be there Friday evening."

"I'll have supper waiting for you," she promised him.

"I'd like to talk to the children now" was his response.

As conversations went, it was one of the coldest, most formal ones she had ever taken part in. But Ryan was coming home, and she could make her plans. That would have to be good enough.

On Friday morning, all the children packed overnight bags and put them in the van. Then Stacey drove them to the Finlaws' house. She had already explained that Margie and Ron had invited them to visit for the weekend and that she and Uncle Ryan would stop by on Saturday to see how they were doing. Even Christy was excited until she realized that Stacey was leaving her. When the little girl began to sob, Stacey explained firmly that she had to stay with Margie, but that Stacey would see her the next day.

"I hope this is worth it," Stacey muttered as she drove away, the little girl's sobs ringing in her ears.

Turning the van toward town, Stacey drove into the parking lot of one of Tallahassee's shopping malls. After hours of window shopping, she finally made her purchase, driving next to the beauty salon where she always had her hair trimmed.

There were posters of glamorous young women with various hairstyles all over the front window, and Stacey examined them carefully before going inside. Obviously the trend was for short, spiky haircuts. Taking a look at her reflection in the plate glass, she decided that a change would make her appear more sophisticated. I'm tired of looking like Miss Rural America, she decided defiantly. Maybe a different hairstyle will make me act differently.

Minutes later, as she was actually sitting in the stylist's chair gazing at her long honey hair, try as she might, the words that would initiate the new, radically different Stacey MacDonald Cunningham wouldn't come. Half an hour later, she emerged with only her straggly ends clipped. Unless there were a tape measure handy, no one would know that she had even had her hair cut. "I'm such a coward," she groaned as she got into the van. "I'll never change."

A stop at the grocery store for dinner supplies and champagne completed her shopping trip. Mrs. Watson was just leaving when Stacey arrived. "Thanks," Stacey called to her.

The house was gleaming, its sparkle impossible to miss, since there was almost no furniture in it to impede the view. Stacey moved a wooden crate indoors to substitute for a coffee table in the living room, and she placed the two small floor pillows on either side of it. There were wild flowers blooming across the driveway; after picking a large bouquet, she set it in a hand-blown mason jar to decorate the crate. An antique tin bucket sat on the tile hearth of the fireplace, filled with a bag of ice and one very expensive bottle of champagne.

An hour later the kitchen smelled of *boeuf bourguignon*, which was simmering slowly on the stove. A green salad was stored in the refrigerator waiting only to be tossed, and French bread resided in the oven waiting to be warmed up. Beautiful whole strawberries were washed and draining on the sink for dessert.

Stacey climbed the stairs to her bedroom and undressed quickly. It was getting late and Ryan's biggest surprise was yet to come. She ran a hot bath and filed her nails as the tub filled. Even though she would have loved to linger, she bathed quickly, splashing herself afterward with a floral cologne.

Wrapped in a towel, she went back to her room and opened the box from the expensive boutique she had visited earlier that day. Such a lot of money for so little, she lamented as she removed the price tag from the little scrap of coffee-colored silk. She held it over her head and let the fabric slither down over her breasts and waist. As she had guessed, it hid absolutely nothing. The neckline plunged almost to her navel, and when she moved the material swayed loosely over her breasts, exposing every detail. The hem just skimmed the top of the matching bikini pants, and all the edges were richly bordered with black lace.

This is definitely not me, she decided as she looked in the mirror after applying subtly enhancing makeup; the thought was pleasing. Rummaging through her suitcases, which she had so far refused to unpack, she found a black cloisonné comb, which she used to pull her hair back from her face and fasten it on one side of her head. A small pair of gold hoop earrings completed the picture.

There was a matching black lace robe that Stacey slipped on before she went downstairs. Since the robe hid nothing, the effect was not diminished. Well, she thought, taking one last look, if Ryan doesn't get the idea, then we really are in trouble.

It was six-thirty, and Stacey began to suffer an attack of terminal butterflies. To counteract her nervousness, she busied herself setting up the stereo system that had been moved from the condominium. Since there were no shelves to hold it, she set the pieces of equipment in a row along the wall beside the fireplace. Looking carefully through Ryan's collection of tapes, she chose Rimsky-Korsakov's *Scheherazade* for predinner music and Ravel's *Bolero* for afterward. We can't miss, she gloated.

By seven-thirty the *boeuf bourguignon* was done, and the heat had been turned off beneath it. Stacey busied herself fluffing the two floor pillows and mopping up the leak from the tin bucket of rapidly melting ice. Starving, she finally sampled the crackers and port-wine cheese that she had set out for an appetizer. Reclining on the pillows against the wall, she turned on the tape deck.

By eight-thirty she was upset enough to call Ryan's emergency number. If this doesn't rate as an emergency, she growled to herself, nothing does. I'm about to plot a murder. The number had the same area code as that of Tallahassee, and Stacey realized as she dialed that Ryan was somewhere in northern Florida. He could have gotten home by now, she reasoned, even if he had waited until five o'clock to start out.

The phone rang for a long time; just as Stacey was about to hang up, a female voice with a North Carolina drawl answered. "Hello," Stacey said, not allowing her shock to show in her voice. "May I speak to Ryan Cunningham, please?"

"Oh, I'm so sorry, honey." The voice didn't sound sorry at all. "Mr. Ryan Cunningham is entirely too busy to answer phone calls right now. He just can't be disturbed." There was a whispered conversation that Stacey couldn't make out, and then the voice came back on the line. "Let me take your name and he'll get back to you when he's not so preoccupied." A nauseating giggle followed, and Stacey, gripping the phone so hard her knuckles were white, almost hung up.

A spark of pride surfaced just as she was dropping the receiver into the cradle, and she swung the receiver back to her ear. "Yes, MyraLou," she said calmly. "Please tell

Ryan that Stacey Cun—that Stacey MacDonald called. And tell him for me, will you, that I'm glad somebody else wants him. I sure don't!'' She hung up quickly, her shaking fingers barely able to find the right place to drop the receiver.

I am not going to cry, she decided as she wandered through the house kicking her bare toes against the newly plastered walls. Ryan was having a spectacular time; why should she sit there and cry over what never was? She stubbed her toe with a particularly vicious kick and tears of pain sprang to her eyes. What am I doing? she wondered. I should be celebrating. I've got all the trimmings: champagne, a gourmet dinner. I've got the rest of this miserable night to get through.

When Stacey went back to the living room, she found that the champagne was still cold even though most of the ice had melted. Resolutely, she sat down on the bunched pillows and popped the cork. "To me," she toasted. "And to the marvelously adaptable man I married." Unable to find wineglasses, she had set out water tumblers. She poured a full glass of the sparkling beverage, holding it high in the air. "May the rest of our marriage be carried out as far from each other as possible." She clicked her glass against the empty one sitting on the crate. "Here's to you, Ryan," she said, draining the entire glass in one long series of swallows.

The wine affected her empty stomach like a meteor shower. That's better, she thought with satisfaction. The new feeling gave her something to think about other than her misery. If one glass made her feel that different, two would feel even better. She quickly drained another glass. "Better still," she muttered.

Sliding off the pillows, she stood up and walked in circles around the living room carrying the dripping bottle by its slippery neck. Finally she wandered into the kitchen to look at her stew, which had cooled down and separated into greasy layers. She stuck it, pot and all, into the refrigerator next to the salad. Leaning against the kitchen counter, she plopped two strawberries into a Pluto Pup drinking glass that belonged to Jonathan and filled it to the top with more champagne. "How decadent." She giggled. The words sounded as though they were being spoken through a paper bag.

"Am I getting drunk?" She giggled again. "Nah, sweet Stacey MacDonald, professional virgin and Earth Mother, would never get drunk." She hiccuped. "You can't get drunk on..." she held up the bottle and squinted narrowly at it, "...two-thirds of a bottle of champagne."

Stacey popped two more strawberries into her mouth. "Just in case," she muttered, shaking a long finger at her nose. Somewhere a still-rational voice reminded her that she had skipped lunch that day too. She popped another strawberry. "There—what a good girl am I!"

Filling Pluto Pup with the last of the champagne, she wove her way back into the living room. "How convenient not to have furniture," she crowed. "Nothing to stumble over."

Flicking on the tape deck, she finished the contents of her glass and flopped tummy down on the pillow. The haunting strains of *Bolero* began. "Why did Ravel want to repeat the same thing over and over again?" she wondered out loud. "The poor guy probably couldn't think of anything else to write."

Something about her words sounded familiar. She concentrated on figuring out why. A glimmer of understanding shot through her spinning head. She and Ravel were just alike. They kept trying to make it big, but they only ended up repeating the same theme again and again.

Neither of us, she mourned silently, neither of us is capable of a single bit of originality. For him, it's the same old dum, da da dum, da da dum dum, dum...and for me? She thought for a moment, her foggy brain grasping for the connection. "Ah, yes," she muttered groggily. "For me, it's trying to make love out of nothing at all. Over and over and over and..." The sadness of it brought tears to her eyes, and she wiped them on the hem of the black lace robe.

The tears continued to fall and she sniffled repeatedly as the music crashed through her. "Poor Ravel," she said as she wept. "Poor, poor Ravel." She sat up and leaned precariously against the wall. But as the music got louder, she let herself slide slowly down again, inch by inch, until finally her head was lying on the pillow and her long legs and scantily clad body were on the bare floor.

"Poor, poor Ravel.... Poor, poor Georgia gal...." Her eyes fluttered shut, diamond teardrops on her long eyelashes, as finally the tape deck clicked off and she drifted into unconsciousness.

"Stacey, you little fool, what in heaven's name are you doing undressed and asleep on the cold floor?" Large, strong hands were shaking her and she tried to respond, but her eyes seemed to be sewn shut. She managed a moan, and even that made her head spin.

"Are you sick?" The hands were smoothing her hair back from her forehead and checking her for fever. She moaned again.

"You're not hot. Do you hurt anywhere?"

"Stop shouting," she managed to say, flinging her arms over her eyelids to protect them from the light. Was it daytime already?

"Can you sit up?" The man was still shouting, and she put her finger up to her mouth.

"Shhhh," she whispered. "Stacey is sleeping. Go away."

"You're drunk as a cat in a beer barrel. What got into you?"

"One very good bottle of champagne." She giggled and then moaned at the pain it caused.

"A whole bottle?"

"What's it to you?" she muttered. Cautiously she strained to open one eye. The man leaning over her came slowly into focus. "You don't have to worry, Ryan," she grumbled. "I bought it with my own money."

"Stacey, do you have a drinking problem?"

Her other eye opened, and she blinked incredulously at him. The total irony of the question ripped through her in waves of painful giggles. "Absolutely. I have a real problem drinking anything stronger than soda pop. I don't like the taste. You should see the problem I cause at parties." The giggles continued to flow through her, leaving her body weak and her head pounding.

"It's not funny." His voice was deadly, and it knocked the laughter right out of her.

"You're funny, Ryan," she managed to say finally. "You come home a day late, after who knows what kind of perverted activities, and you question me about my morals?"

"A day late? You must be drunk." His voice was as hard as an anvil.

Gritting her teeth, she managed to sit up, holding her head in her hands. "What day is it?" she asked with as much dignity as she could manage.

"It's Friday night. Nine-thirty, to be exact."

"That's not possible," she spat at him. "Not unless you've just been in Quincy all this time."

"I've been in Jacksonville all this time."

"That's a three-hour drive." She lifted her aching head and watched the room undulate around her. "I called your little emergency number an hour ago and MyraLou said you were there, only she didn't want me to disturb you."

"You really must be smashed." Ryan was regarding her with an expression that could freeze Lake Erie. "MyraLou lives in North Carolina, not Jacksonville. Your befuddled brain misplaced that information somehow. I left Jacksonville at four-thirty but, fool that I am, I drove so fast to get here that I was nailed for speeding.

I've spent the last two hours paying fines and getting myself out of a Podunk Florida jail.''

"She had a North Carolina accent. She said that you couldn't be disturbed." Tears of bewilderment were streaming down Stacey's aching face. She tried to brush them away, but her hand couldn't find the right place.

Ryan's expression changed, warming up a degree or two. "The contractor I've been working with is married to a three-hundred-pound Southern belle. It's their number that I gave you. Unfortunately, she's a real ding-dong. I told her that I was going home to be with my wife and that I wasn't to be disturbed this weekend for anything. She obviously took me literally."

Compute, brain, compute. Stacey strained to put together the facts. One thing was indisputable. Ryan was there. If the clock really said nine-thirty, and his car was really in the driveway, he was telling the truth. "Let me see your watch," she said, dropping her eyes to his wrist. Had it been anything but a digital, she couldn't have managed to decipher it. But even her bleary eyes could see the bright red digits. 9:38.

With every ounce of strength that she still possessed, Stacey stumbled to the doorway. Ryan's car was parked near the front door. Sagging against the door frame, she turned her head. He was right behind her.

"Well?"

"Ryan," she began haltingly, "you've got to admit, at least when I blow it, I blow it good." Then she passed out in his arms.

There were warm arms around her holding her close to a lean, masculine body, and a hairy leg was thrown over hers, pinning her to the sheets, when she awoke again. It was easier this time to open her eyes, although not much, and she lay still, trying to remember where she was. Whom she was with was much easier.

"Good morning, Georgia peach."

Her mouth was as dry as a desert mirage, and she swallowed twice before she could speak. "I hope so," she murmured.

"Do you know where you are?"

A cautious appraisal of the room informed her that she was in Ryan's bedroom. "Yes."

"Do you know what happened last night?"

Her heart thudded against her chest like a Great Dane wagging its tail. "Up to a point."

Ryan moved away from her and with one sure motion, rolled her onto her back. In a split second, his muscular body was half covering her soft one. He was naked and so was she. She gasped so hard that the rush of air into her lungs was like a bellows. The sudden movement also brought into focus just how much her head was aching.

Ryan saw her whiten and he laughed, his mouth only a kiss away from hers. "You had this all planned, didn't you, Georgia peach? You brought me home from Jacksonville just so you could seduce me."

He was right, but the circumstances that she had imagined had been much different. Still, now was better than never. Gingerly she nodded her head, unable to look any higher than his chin.

"Well, it was wonderful. Simply fabulous. I've never spent a more memorable night in my life."

Her eyes shot up to stare into his, which were glinting like coals in the morning sunlight. "You mean..." She realized, suddenly, how insulting it would be if she told him that she didn't remember his lovemaking. "You mean...I was that good?" The lie made her miserable, and she dropped her eyes again.

"Good? Honey, you were breathtaking."

"I'm...I'm glad."

"And now, Stacey dearest, I want you to show me everything you learned last night. Just the way we talked about it." Ryan's eyes were shadowed, and there was an edge to his voice that she didn't understand.

She lay still, trying to puzzle out the night before, trying desperately to remember. There was no hope of it, she simply had no idea what to do. "I can't really remember what we said," she hedged. "Can you refresh my memory?"

Ryan's mouth descended to hers, tasting with great sensitivity. "Does that remind you?" he asked, withdrawing slightly to watch her eyes.

"A little."

"Let's try again." This time the kiss was one of grinding passion and his hand traveled over her soft curves, stopping at her thighs. "Come on, Stacey. Perform for me. You have nothing to be afraid of now."

Grimly she did as she was told, trying not to jump when he began to explore her warmth. He stopped as he felt her stiffen. "Why, Stacey. You're acting like a virgin again."

Tears gathered in her eyes, and she wiped them away quickly with her fists. "Ryan," she pleaded. "I don't remember anything about last night. I'm so sorry. Please be gentler with me."

She felt his body tighten against hers for a moment, and his curls brushed her cheek. Then he rolled over and she was free of his weight. "No, I'm the one who's sorry, Georgia gal," he muttered. "I was trying to hurt you the way I've been hurt. Only there's no pleasure in it."

They lay beside each other, not touching. Stacey waited for him to speak. "Stacey," he said finally, "nothing happened last night. I carried you up here and put you in my bed in case you needed anything during the night. You were really out of it. We both slept; that's all."

This news was even more of a shock than his announcement that they had consummated their marriage had been. "Why did you tell me differently? Why did you hurt me like that?"

Ryan sat up, his long expanse of back visible and, even under the circumstances, tantalizing. "I'm tired of being played for a fool, Georgia gal. I came home last night expecting reconciliation. Hell, there hasn't been anything to reconcile, has there? Anyway, I find you so full of Dutch courage you can't see straight. Is that what it takes to make love to your husband, Stacey? Did you think a bottle of champagne would make it bearable?"

He stood up, naked and gracefully masculine, and bent over to pick up the jeans from the floor beside the bed. "Nice try. I was tempted, even under the circumstances, to take you up on your pitiful offer, but what little self-control I still possess stopped me." She heard the rasp of the zipper and then he turned to face her. "If you and I are going to maintain this facade of a marriage, there will be no more attempts like last night. Do you understand?"

"Why do you keep trying to misunderstand?" she asked him quietly. She was sitting up in bed now, with the covers pulled loosely around her breasts and her hair tumbled around her shoulders. One hoop earring tickled her cheek as she shook her head. "I think, Ryan, that you want to believe I don't need you the way a woman needs a man. Maybe that will make it easier for you to move back into the fast lane. After all, if we have no relationship, you'll never have to worry about hurting me."

His sarcastic snort filled her ears, but she pressed on. "Well, I have one thing to say that you'll find even more amusing. Let this thought echo in your head, Ryan, when you're off kicking up your heels. I used to think I loved you; I used to think that holding you in my arms would be life's ultimate joy. Now I think I'll be glad to be rid of you."

With a serenity that she didn't feel, Stacey got up from the bed, gloriously naked, and walked to the door. "Take a good look, Florida boy. It's the last one you'll ever get." The slam that followed her into the hall almost ripped the door off its hinges.

Chapter Eleven

There was a rooster crowing and the smell of new-mown hay in the air. Slowly Stacey opened her eyes and let her surroundings penetrate her consciousness. As it had every morning since she had left Tallahassee, reality came into focus very slowly. The bed was familiar, the pink walls of the room were the same as they had always been; she was in Georgia again.

Turning on her side, she looked at the two little girls asleep in the corner on her sisters' beds. Caroline and Christy were motionless, dreaming pleasant dreams, or at least it seemed that they were. Caroline had a tiny smile on her face, and Christy, who had been fretful the first few nights after their arrival, was making up for lost time by sleeping heavily.

They were just beginning to get used to the new house, and I moved them again, Stacey thought with the same guilty pang that had struck her every day for the entire week since they had left the house in Tallahassee. Actually, the children had adjusted nicely, taking at face value Stacey's explanation that Mrs. MacDonald needed some help with the summer's canning and freezing. Their only complaint was that they hadn't seen their uncle in such a long time.

"We've all been invited to visit for a week," she had told them on Saturday morning after she had thrown her suitcases in the van and driven them all immediately to Margie's house. "Your Uncle Ryan had to go back to work right away, and he won't be home for at least another week. I think we'll have a good time in Georgia."

In truth, Stacey had no idea what Ryan's plans were. He had left immediately after their fight, and Stacey had wasted no time in following suit. Without so much as a note explaining her actions, she had locked up the house and fled. Margie had tried desperately to get her to discuss her decision, but Stacey had refused, packing the children in the van as calmly as she could. Fervently hoping that she was not communicating her state of mind to them, she had driven to Georgia, stopping only for necessities and one quick phone call to inform her parents of their arrival.

She had chosen not to share her real reason for the visit with her folks—airing dirty linen was not her style—but Stacey was sure that her mother suspected that she and Ryan were having problems. Alternately keeping Stacey busy with myriad farm chores and giving her ample free time for long walks, Mrs. MacDonald let her daughter know that she wanted to help.

The children had been made right at home. Stacey's siblings taught them farm survival skills, letting them milk cows, gather eggs, and hoe weeds in the vegetable garden. Stacey's sisters filled the old truck with bales of hay and drove the children for miles on an impromptu hay ride. James and Randy tied a rope to the barn rafters and showed the kids how to jump out of the hay loft while holding tightly onto the rope, one foot in a sturdy loop.

Stacey watched with gratitude, glad for once that she did not have to take charge of the children herself. Like a dog licking its wounds, she had allowed herself to withdraw, plodding through each day in a pain-filled fog.

One week, she thought as she listened to the rooster crow again. It's been exactly one week since I left. She couldn't wait any longer; she had to take the children back to Florida the next day. School would be starting soon.

Rising, she dressed in faded jeans and a shapeless T-shirt, a castoff of one of her sisters. Lethargically she pulled a comb through her hair and tied the laces of a pair of worn sneakers. Today was tomato-canning day. Tomorrow was the end of her marriage.

By suppertime she and her mother and two of her four sisters had canned enough tomatoes to last the family until summer arrived again. "I'm going to take a shower and go for a walk," Stacey told her mother.

Mrs. MacDonald, who believed that skipping a meal went against the Ten Commandments, just patted her hand. "Sure, honey. Only..." She looked at Stacey's outfit. "When you get out of the shower, put on something more presentable. If you look nice, maybe you'll feel better."

Stacey, who was beyond quick-fix cures for her psyche, forced herself to nod her head. After the shower she put on turquoise slacks and a matching cotton pullover sweater. It wouldn't help her, but it might make her mother feel better. Waving good-bye to her family, she set off across a corn field to walk through the woods at the edge of her parents' property.

Each one of the MacDonald children had a special place where he or she would go when being part of a large, noisy family became too much to deal with. Stacey's special place had always been a clump of trees in the center of the woods. There was a certain feel to the spot, a rightness about it that had always appealed to her, soothing her when she needed soothing. The trees, five of them, grew in a circle. In the center of the circle was a mound of stones that Stacey, as a young teenager, had hauled there.

She had carefully transplanted wild flowers too, and although most of them had not lived more than a day or two, some of them had dug their roots tenaciously into the ground and dropped their seeds for future generations. Today flowers still bloomed, and somehow the sight of that much dedication, that much persistence, was a reminder to her of her own failures.

She was no closer to knowing what to do about her marriage than she had been a week before. But her own uncertainty was academic. By now, the decision had probably been made. By Ryan.

Although Stacey was sure that Ryan knew where she was, he had made no attempt to get in touch with her. So much anger, she thought sadly. So many misunderstandings. There is no road back for us now.

It could have been different. So very different. She clasped her arms across her chest, protecting herself against the imaginary chill in the air. Carefully, she picked her way across the wildflower carpet to sit on a stone. "I don't want to destroy your friends," she murmured to a lone daisy by her side. "I've destroyed enough for a lifetime."

There had been so many assumptions, so much incorrect information, so much miscommunication. "How could two mature adults screw up so badly?" she asked the daisy. "Heaven knows, I think we were both trying."

"That's a good question," said a husky voice behind her. "I've been asking myself the same thing."

Daisies, even daisies in special places, didn't talk. For that matter, neither did trees. Stacey twisted to face the man leaning against a tall poplar. As always, the sight of Ryan sent messages crashing to each of her nerve endings. He looked the same, although he had cut his hair since she had last seen him, and there were lines around his eyes that seemed unfamiliar.

"And what answers have you come up with?" she asked him, her voice a forest whisper, an imitation of the wind sighing through the tall pine trees.

"That we can't go on hurting each other anymore. That neither of us should have to live with this pain."

Somehow, when she had imagined Ryan asking her to annul their marriage, she had expected anger or perhaps pity. She had not expected the gentleness, the concern, that she saw in his eyes. It made it harder to find the words she had to say.

She was grateful when he rescued her. "Don't say anything now." He pushed away from the poplar and walked toward her, holding out his hand to help her stand up. "My car is parked out on the road. We'll talk later."

She followed him through the forest. Strangely, he had not dropped her hand but had tucked it under his arm as he led her along the leaf-padded path. Whatever happens, she thought, whatever he has decided, he's going to be kind about it. And Ryan kind was going to be harder to deal with than Ryan angry.

They walked up the road and Ryan held the car door open for her. Instead of turning toward the house, he continued in the direction the car had been pointing. Assuming they were going into town to find a place to sit and drink and discuss the sordid details, Stacey shut her eyes and leaned back in the comfortable seat. "You knew where to find me, so you must have talked to my mother. Did you see the children?"

"They hadn't come back from swimming in your neighbor's pond."

"They've missed you." She opened her eyes and turned her head but watching him was too painful. He had never looked better to her, she thought. He was dressed casually and there was a slight ridge over his nose where his sunglasses had rested, and never had he looked more handsome, more male. She wanted to smooth the new lines from around his eyes and run her finger down the sharp contours of his face. She wanted to brush his curls over his forehead and tickle his earlobe with her tongue and with her teeth. Instead she closed her eyes.

"I'll see them soon," he said, his tone noncommittal. "I've missed them."

It was taking a long time to get to town, and finally Stacey opened her eyes. She recognized the stretch of road. They were not going to Gainesville. "Where are we going, Ryan?" she asked as she continued to stare out the window.

"Under the circumstances this may be hard for you to do, but I want you to trust me, Georgia gal. You'll know soon enough. Just make yourself comfortable."

Amazingly she did. With a certain grim fatality she settled herself against the cushions and closed her eyes again. There was a whole week of restless nights in her immediate past, and she was very tired. There seemed to be nothing she could do to turn the tide of their lives. With the sense of one burden having been lifted from her shoulders, even if it was to be replaced soon with a heavier one, she fell sound asleep.

She slept and slept, trying once or twice to pull herself back into consciousness with no success. The motion of the car, her exhaustion, and the stillness around her were just too potent. It was only when the air she was breathing began to change, when it cooled and thinned so that her lungs had to readjust, that she opened her eyes.

They were in the mountains and it was dark. But there were stars overhead and a three-quarter moon that cast enough light to see the ghostly ancient oaks and the skeletons of rhododendrons. Why?

She had agreed to trust Ryan, but her heart was flip-flopping at his choice of a place to hold their last conversation. Why?

There were silent tears running down her cheeks, and she wiped them away with her fingertips. "Don't cry, Stacey," Ryan's voice broke the stillness. It was a gentle command, and she took a deep breath before she turned to look at him.

"Why, Ryan?"

"Trust me just a little longer. Can you do that for me?"

She nodded. With his face silvered by the moonlight, every shadow, every curve and indentation, spoke of strength and raw-boned masculinity. I want him so much, she thought despairingly. I want him forever. I still love him just as much as I did...more.

She knew where they were going now. They passed quickly through Highlands, taking the back road toward Cashiers where the cabin was located. They passed only an occasional car; the road was deserted for long stretches. It was spectacular, even at night. Once she heard the sound of rushing water and she remembered the day at the rock slide. We were happy then, she thought. Why, Ryan? Why here?

The car made it up the steep driveway, coming to rest in front of the log cabin. Ryan turned off the motor and they sat looking at the moon illuminating the steep roof. In the distance the granite slopes of Whiteside Mountain shone out of the darkness.

Finally Ryan got out and came around to open her door. It was a gentlemanly courtesy in which he usually didn't indulge—there had always been children to get out of seats and luggage or groceries to haul in. The gesture made her feel very feminine, and for a moment she pretended they were really lovers, extending the small tokens of affection lovers extend to each other.

She swung her legs to the ground as Ryan stood in front of her. As she stood up, he reached to help her, circling her waist with his hands. When she was firmly planted on the rocky ground, she expected him to step back, but he didn't.

"Your hair changes color in the moonlight." He lifted a hand and brushed a long strand away from her face. "I never know what color to call it. Just when I think I've figured it out, it changes."

"It's brown." She sighed, wishing his hand would brush her cheek again. "Just brown."

"No, it's gold in the sunlight, and under the moon it's dark honey. I love the feel of it." He lifted both hands to her face, framing it for a moment before he wove his fingers into the long strands and tunneled his hands through the whole shining mass. Exerting slight pressure, he pulled her to rest against the buttons of his shirt. "Do you have any idea, Georgia gal, how much I've wanted to see this hair spread out on the pillow beside me?"

She was shaking; every inch of her body was trembling from wanting the same thing. "Oh, Ryan," she said brokenly.

"Do you have any idea, Georgia gal, just how much I've wanted you to run every silky strand over my chest as you lay on top of me caressing me with your soft, lovely hands...?"

She was weeping again in big, broken sobs. Ryan held her close, stroking her back through the thin material of her sweater. Finally, he framed her face again, drawing it up to meet his eyes. Gently he bent and kissed the only tear she hadn't wiped away on the hem of his shirt. "Come up to the porch with me. I want to talk to you."

His arm was around her, pulling her up the walk with him, but she held back, sustaining the closeness as long as she could. She had no faith in their ability to solve their massive problems with a conversation, and she didn't want to hear what Ryan would surely tell her anyway.

He settled her on the porch swing, then squeezed in next to her, his arm around her shoulders. He was going to be kind, understanding even, and when the evening was done, she would not be able to hate him for ending their attempt at marriage. They would part as friends; perhaps, if he retained custody of the children, she would even be allowed to visit. The pain that wrenched through her at the thought caused her to shudder in protest.

"Do I affect you so negatively that you can't sit next to me without shuddering in distaste?" No longer kind, his voice was strained.

Another misunderstanding. This could not go on. No matter what passed between them, she would not allow him to leave believing that she had not wanted him. Let him live with the real truth in the quiet hours of his life after she was gone.

"You're a fool, Ryan Cunningham. You've purposely misconstrued everything that has happened between us. From the beginning, I've wanted you so badly I couldn't see straight. I want you now even more." She moved away from him, just far enough to see his face. "I'm sure it would be nicer if I let you believe otherwise, but I'm not feeling heroic tonight. Go ahead and end this farce, but don't kid yourself. Do it for the right reasons. Do it because you don't love me, never did, and never will. Do it because we've both realized that a marriage of convenience is hell."

On the porch the moonlight was muted, iridescent, but even in the near darkness, Stacey could read his expression. Still, she couldn't understand it.

"Georgia gal, did you think I brought you all the way to North Carolina to end our marriage?"

She watched him as he lifted a hand to her face, tracing the smooth skin under her eyes, around her nose. "Yes," she said uncertainly. "Didn't you?"

"Not unless that's what you want."

She stared at him, and she still didn't understand. "It would be terrible for the kids if we annulled this marriage," she said uncertainly.

"Absolutely terrible," he agreed.

"And their aunt could sue for custody..."

"She certainly could...would, in fact."

"My family is crazy about all of you. They'd never forgive me."

"Never."

"I'd be the first MacDonald to end a marriage. By annullment, yet."

"After tonight, Georgia gal, there will be no hope of an annullment."

His words stunned her into silence. Eyes like a full moon stared back at him, and very slowly he grinned at her.

"You still want me?" she said in a small voice. "Even after all the times that haven't worked out for us." Her voice broke, and she flung herself at his chest. "Oh, Ryan, I'm so terribly sorry."

He soothed her by stroking her hair, finally pulling her onto his lap. "Stop, Georgia peach. It's all right; it's not your fault. Margie told me the whole story. I'm the one who's sorry."

"For what?" She sniffed. "For wanting me and having me refuse you time after time."

"Only twice," he corrected her. "The third time you were very willing, only you were unconscious."

She groaned, leaning her head against his shirt. The buttons pressed uncomfortably into her cheek. Without thinking, she moved her head away and began to unfasten them, stroking her hands down the springy curls on his chest as she uncovered them. Finally she laid her head back down, her silky hair falling like a veil over him. "If you had come home even an hour earlier that night, our lives would be so much different now." Wrapping her hands behind his back, she began to trace each separate muscle, each section of his spine.

"Do you have any idea what you're doing?"

"Certainly I do. I'm not unconscious now." Her mouth found two matching places to explore and she nuzzled them, excitement growing at his groaning response.

"Stop that, Georgia gal. We have to finish our conversation."

"I don't think it's our conversation that we have to finish," she said sweetly. "It's not our conversation that keeps getting interrupted."

"Margie called me every name in the book for not being more patient, more sensitive with you. She said I was a dirty, lecherous man who didn't deserve to be your first lover. If she could see you now."

Stacey sat up, leaning against his chest as she looked straight into his eyes. "She's absolutely crazy. I love you, dirty, lecherous man that you are. Don't change!"

Ryan's mouth merged with hers. Whose lips opened first, whose tongue explored initially, would forever remain a mystery. Finally Ryan pushed her gently away. "Slow down there. We have all night, and I intend to take hours with you, love."

She started at the endearment and he noticed her rapid blinking. "Yes," he whispered in her ear. "Don't you know?"

She shook her head shyly. "Please tell me," she implored softly. "I need to hear it. It will make tonight perfect."

"Well, once upon a time," he started slowly and then laughed as she pummeled his chest. "I told you I was going to take hours warming you up, Anastasia Elizabeth; this is just for openers." He grasped her hands and placed them, palms down on his chest. "Now, where was I...?"

"Ryan," she warned.

"Yes, now I remember. Once upon a time, I walked into a room and fell in love. There was a vision dressed in green gingham with wilting daisies in her hair standing across the room, and I knew that I was lost."

"Me too, only it was Tom Sawyer for me." She ran her tongue over the most sensitive places on his neck and then laughed softly at his groan.

"You can whitewash my fence anytime you want." He dropped a kiss on her hair, and his voice got serious. "The trouble was that I had nothing to offer this vision. Who in their right mind would want to marry a man with four children?"

"Me," she murmured.

"Yes, and when I discovered that, I thought it was the only reason you were marrying me. But your responses before we took our vows were encouraging. I thought if I could make love to you, over and over, and let you know how much I cared for you, perhaps you'd fall in love with me too."

"I've always loved you." Her eyes filled with tears. She was going to dehydrate completely if this kept up.

"I had no idea in the world. On our wedding night you were so lovely, I couldn't be patient. I settled for being gentle instead. It wasn't enough; you needed more."

"I needed a room away from my adolescent brothers!"

Ryan's hands had been stroking her back under the sweater, but suddenly they were still. "What?"

She was silent. The entire fiasco of their wedding night came back to her in a rush. Finally she ventured, "Didn't Margie tell you about that?"

"No."

"James and Randy were listening to us. They could hear every sound, every gasp, every creak of the bed springs. I just couldn't handle it. I felt as if we were on display!"

Ryan's chest began to rumble. Expecting sympathy, Stacey was astounded. He was laughing. "Ryan..." she said murderously.

"I'm sorry." He choked. "I'm very sorry...." Suddenly she was laughing too. It felt so good to laugh with him, to feel his body shaking against hers, to know that Ryan wasn't angry.

"Poor Anastasia Elizabeth..." he murmured finally, when he had regained control of himself. "My poor, poor love. I had no idea."

"We've made some very bad decisions," Stacey mused. "Trying to celebrate our wedding night in a house crowded with people, trying again when we had a sick child in the house..."

"I feel especially bad about that," Ryan interrupted. "I thought you were using Christy as an excuse. Margie told me that she was really sick."

"I wasn't looking for excuses, Ryan. The night you came home from Jacksonville, I had planned in great detail just how to seduce you."

"Yes, and when I came in and found you spread out on the floor wearing almost nothing, I panicked like a drowning man. I thought you were sick—or worse, I thought someone else had discovered you first. The house was wide open and the stereo was still on—I was so frightened." He shook her gently. "Don't ever take chances like that again," he reprimanded her.

She kissed his worried frown, smoothing the furrows with her tongue. They were finished with apologies, with explanations. The night was ahead of them, and yet Stacey could feel his hesitation. There had been too much rejection, too many disappointments.

"Ryan," she whispered against his forehead. "If a train comes through the cabin, or an orphanage of tubercular children comes to the door begging, or I'm seized with an attack of appendicitis, don't stop loving me tonight. I need you. Now, Ryan."

It was all he needed. His hands tugged at the bottom of her sweater, turning it inside out as he slowly inched it over her head. Her lacy bra was unhooked and followed it to the ground below the swing. Still, Ryan was in no hurry, feeling each glorious inch of her back as she lay in his arms. Finally, he lightly brushed his thumbs against the soft sides of her breasts and advanced to the velvety skin beneath them. When he lightly flicked the rosy tips with his thumbnails, she groaned.

"Ryan, don't take hours," she implored him. "Take me now, before something happens."

"Oh, something is going to happen, all right," he told her in a husky voice. "I can promise you that something is definitely going to happen."

"I can't stand waiting," she whimpered as his mouth descended to taste the rigid fruits of his exploration.

"Anastasia Elizabeth, you are going to be amazed at what you can stand." She sank her hands into his dark curls as he lifted her and carried her across the porch. He turned the doorknob, shoving the unlocked door open with his hip. The cabin was dark, but the moon shining through the windows showed them the way to the loft steps.

Ryan carried her slowly and set her gently on the bed. There were candles, which he took his time lighting, and flowers in jars on the floor. The bed was smooth beneath her, and Ryan when he came to her was hard and sure beside her.

"Ryan, please?" she whispered, her tongue exploring the fine whorls of his ear as his hands explored every inch of her body, lingering, teasing, as she writhed beneath him.

"Hours, Georgia peach. We have hours." And she discovered that he was right. She had no idea what she could stand, what joy would be hers. When finally, an aching century later, he covered her body with his and made them one, the power of it, the sheer magnificence of the act, made her weep. Ryan kissed away the tears as he taught her how to pleasure them both. She moved beneath him in wonder, her daydreams disappearing to be replaced with glorious reality. When at last she was his completely, she knew that she could stand no more happiness, that she was full, bursting with more love than she had ever imagined she could hold.

Later they lay entwined, candlelight flickering over their glowing bodies. Stacey traced the angles of Ryan's chest with the ends of her hair, glad she had left it long enough to be able to caress him.

"This was the perfect place for it to happen." She sighed in contentment. "It was so thoughtful of you to rent it for our honeymoon."

"Buy it. It was so thoughtful of me to buy it," he corrected her.

She sat up in a daze, carelessly naked beside him. "You didn't!"

He pulled her down to his chest, her hair hanging down around them. "For you, Georgia peach, just for you. It's my wedding present. I came up yesterday, signed all the papers, and put it in your name. I love our kids, and I love our house in Florida. But this one is just for us. When life looms too large for us to remember what we mean to each other, we'll come here."

Her eyes shone in the flickering light, reflections of the wavering candles. "You've made me so happy."

"In more ways than one," he teased her, his hands traveling lightly over her soft curves.

"I think you're about to make me happy again," she said, smiling shyly at him. "I'm not innocent anymore, you know; I can read the signs."

"Keep reading them, my love. And I'll keep reading yours. Let there be no more misunderstandings between us."

"I think we understand each other perfectly," she whispered, bending over within an inch of his mouth.

"But I think that we should continue practicing. Tell me, do you like this?" She nibbled softly on his bottom lip. "And this?" She placed a line of tiny kisses across his chin.

He rolled over, taking her with him until he was lying on top of her. "You're doing fine. And now it's my turn to find out if we're communicating."

She gave herself up to his embrace. "I love you, Ryan," she whispered, "and I know you love me. I think we'll always remember that. No matter what else we say or do."

"That may be true," he murmured before his mouth took hers, "but I intend to tell you every day of my life. Just to be sure." The moonlight covered them, illuminating their interlaced bodies for just a moment before the last candle flickered out. "Just to be sure," he whispered in the darkness.

READERS' COMMENTS ON SILHOUETTE ROMANCES:

"The best time of my day is when I put my children to bed at naptime and sit down to read a Silhouette Romance. Keep up the good work."

P.M.*, Allegan, MI

"I am very fond of the quality of your Silhouette Romances. They are so real. I have tried to read some of the other romances, but I always come back to Silhouette."

C.S., Mechanicsburg, PA

"I feel that Silhouette Books offer a wider choice and/or variety than any of the other romance books available."

R.R., Aberdeen, WA

"I have enjoyed reading Silhouette Romances for many years now. They are light and refreshing. You can always put yourself in the main characters' place, feeling alive and beautiful."

J.M.K., San Antonio, TX

"My boyfriend always teases me about Silhouette Books. He asks me, how's my love life and naturally I say terrific, but I tell him that there is always room for a little more romance from Silhouette."

F.N., Ontario, Canada

*names available on request

You won't want to miss a single one of the heart-felt stories presented by Silhouette Special Edition; and when you take advantage of this special offer, you won't have to.

You'll also receive a FREE subscription to the Silhouette Books Newsletter as long as you remain a member. Each lively issue is filled with news on upcoming titles, interviews with your favorite authors, even their favorite recipes.

To become a home subscriber and receive your first 4 books FREE, fill out and mail the coupon today!

Silhouette Special Edition®

If you're ready for a more sensual, more provocative reading experience...

We'll send you 4 Silhouette Desire novels FREE...

and without obligation

Then, we'll send you six more Silhouette Desire® novels to preview every month for 15 days with absolutely no obligation!

When you decide to keep them, you pay just $1.95 each ($2.25, in Canada), *with no shipping, handling, or additional charges of any kind!*

Silhouette Desire novels are not for everyone. They are written especially for the woman who wants a more satisfying, more deeply involving reading experience.

Silhouette Desire novels take you *beyond* the others and offer real-life drama and romance of successful women in charge of their lives. You'll share precious, private moments and secret dreams... experience every whispered word of love, every ardent touch, every passionate heartbeat.

As a home subscriber, you will also receive FREE, a subscription to the Silhouette Books Newsletter as long as you remain a member. Each issue is filled with news on upcoming titles, interviews with your favorite authors, even their favorite recipes.

And, the first 4 Silhouette Books are absolutely FREE and without obligation, yours to keep! What could be easier...and where else could you find such a satisfying reading experience?

To get your free books, fill out and return the coupon today!

Silhouette 🥚 Desire®

Silhouette Books, 120 Brighton Rd., P.O. Box 5084, Clifton, NJ 07015-5084

Silhouette **Romance**

COMING NEXT MONTH

PLEASE STAND BY—Marie Nicole
Cartoonist Dirk Kilpatrick had created "Abby," the perfect woman.
No one could compete with her...until he met Vinnie. She had all
Abby's charms, with one advantage...she was real.

FORGOTTEN LOVE—Phyllis Halldorson
Could love conquer all? Mercy's husband, Morgan, had lost his
memory, and she was a stranger to him. Perhaps wrapped in her
arms he would remember the love they'd shared.

THE MATTHEWS AFFAIR—Victoria Glenn
Denise's past had left her as skittish as a colt when it came to love,
but Logan wouldn't give up. Slowly he aimed to win her heart.

WITH MARRIAGE IN MIND—Dorothy Cork
Noeline Hastings had resigned herself to marrying her reliable but
boring boyfriend, Andrew. Then she met Justin Fitzroy and realized
that she could never settle for another man.

THE SEA AT DAWN—Laurie Paige
Roth wasn't the kind of man to fall for a woman like Melba. He
was rich and powerful. He wouldn't be attracted to a sensible,
down-to-earth girl...or would he?

CAMERA SHY—Lynnette Morland
Calm, cool and unerringly professional, Carla Copeland had met
her match. Fletcher Arendt sensed the passion lurking beneath her
facade, and he planned to find a way to unleash it.